BOUND BY RUIN

BRUTAL BEAUTY

BOOK THREE

MISTI WILDS

Bound by Ruin

Author's Note

My Brutal Beauty series was originally intended to be a trilogy, but once Thanatos upgraded from a side character to part of the main cast, he demanded more screen time. I am happy to announce that book four —*Born to Riot*—is coming soon. Our grumpy eldest brother needs his happily ever after, too. 🤍

As always, please check the content warnings on my website prior to reading. If you are new to this series, download the free prequel novella *Brutal Beauty* from my website before continuing. (Seriously, you need to read these in order.)

Bound by Ruin ends on a cliffhanger.

RUIN

I'VE NEVER BEEN INSIDE of Celia's boutique before. It's an older building, the bricks on the front weathered with age and the original hardwood floors from when it was first built in the early 1900s. I've seen pictures of it online and walked past once or twice before I met Celia, but I rarely come to this side of town. When I do, it's always at night when every shop on the street is dark and locked up tight.

Even now, her store should be closing for the evening. The Avenue has long since turned out its lights, with most of shops keeping to the early afternoon business hours. Stepping inside the storefront now, however, you wouldn't know that it's supposed to be empty. Soft music plays from the somewhere in the back, a jazz number with a saxophone melody. If what Celia says is correct, Sara should be wrapping up her shift. I'm probably going to scare her, but she's the one who left the front door unlocked. It'll be her fault if she has a heart attack for being careless.

But it'll be my fault if she dies at our father's hands.

I don't usually care about strangers. People get hurt or die every day. Some, even, hurt themselves on purpose. I never understood why someone would do that. Rebel has tried to explain to me that sometimes, when people want to feel in control of their lives, they go to extreme measures to exert whatever control they can—even if that means cutting into their own skin. The pain is a rush, something that they can control when the rest of the world spins out of reach.

Although I'm not convinced that self-harm is therapeutic, I understand the appeal of bleeding something dry.

If you cut deep enough, all the bad seeps out.

I used to tell myself that all of the times my father used to hurt me, that's what he was trying to do. Take out the bad so that the only parts left were the ones he could love. But when he set fire to our family home during the summer I turned twelve, I learned the truth.

He wanted to get rid of me altogether.

Unlike my brothers, I don't care what happens to our father. I don't think about him in the middle of the night. I don't dream about anything—but if I did, it wouldn't be about him or what he's done to us.

I'd dream about the sunrise.

My father, though, still torments my brothers. Not actively—it's not like he's been prowling the streets trying to ruin their lives—but deeper, locked inside their flesh and bone. My high school science teacher used to talk about genetics and how people are mirror images of their parents, and it makes sense.

By killing me, my father could get rid of the parts of himself he couldn't stand to see. I wonder if he would have watched me burn alive to make sure he'd succeeded.

My mother wasn't awake when the fire started. I'm not sure that she ever felt the flames licking her skin and charring her flesh. I tried to drag her outside, but her body was too heavy, and mine was too weak. I collapsed in the smoke, and Rebel had to pull me out.

He went by a different name back then. We all did.

I wonder if Rage or Rebel will choose another one once they become fathers.

I think about that now—what the future will look like. I never used to consider it, too wrapped up in my targets to see anything past their flesh and sinew shredding in my hands. But now I think about Celia and what a baby could mean for us. Mostly, I turn her body over in my head, wondering if I'll be able to catch the moment when she isn't just one soul anymore, but two.

When my brothers slip between her thighs and fill her body with pieces of their own, do their souls intertwine with hers? Or are souls destined to remain separate so that a new one can be stitched together inside of the mother?

I think that Celia will unlock the answer for me, but to do that, she needs to get pregnant first, and our father is standing in the way of me finding answers.

That's why I go inside of Celia's boutique. Not to

find or save Sara. Not to get revenge for destroying my body. Not even to make Celia or my brothers happy.

I'm here for answers that only the future holds.

A future in which my father is nothing more than a memory from my past.

When I step into Celia's office, something metal clicks over my head. Orange sparks rain down, singing my sleeves and floating to the ground below. A liquid on Celia's desk swirls with color, and on the floor below, three red canisters lie on their sides, spilling even more liquid onto the floor. I can't smell it, but I can hear it puddling beneath my boots and feel it stinging my eyes.

Ruin! Get the fuck out of here! Something's not right!

By the time I hear my brother's shout, it's too late. The embers spark, engulfing the room in a blast of heat. I jump backwards out of the office, but I can already feel the flames dancing all around, roaring in my ears, laughing at me.

I can hear my father's crackling laughter and feel his heavy boot on my spine, weighing me down like I'm twelve years old all over again. Helpless. Afraid. Burning.

I open my mouth to breathe, but all I taste is gasoline, and all I hear are screams.

Not my mother's, like I've imagined a thousand times in a thousand burning memories, but Celia's.

I always wanted to hear her scream, but not like this.

Never like this.

Chapter 1

Celia

Blinding flames of blood orange flicker before my eyes, crackling as they threaten to devour not only the business that I've spent years nurturing, but the love I'm only now starting to believe exists. "Rebel!" I twist my wrists and contort my hands, hoping to break free from my handcuffs, but it's no use. I could rub my skin raw, and I still won't make it inside the burning building in time to save them—the scarred man terrified of fire, and the brother who charged into Hell to find him.

"Ruin!" I feel the sob in my chest threatening to break free, but I won't let it. I won't give in to the anguish burning inside my throat, because nothing is over yet. They're both still alive. They *have* to be.

I can't imagine a future without them.

"Celia," Rage calls out, our phone call still running. "Stay with me. I'm on the way. Keep talking."

"I don't—" I tug at my wrist again, hissing as sharp pain radiates down my forearm. "What do you want me to say? They're in there, burning to death!" Quickly, I rummage through the glove box a third time, hoping to find the missing handcuff key and coming up empty. With a frustrated cry, I slam my fist on the dashboard. "You've got to be *kidding* me! I'm going to kill him!"

Rebel just *had* to be heroic. He *had* to cuff me to the car and run after his brother alone. So fucking *stupid* and selfless and—I choke on the emotions overflowing from my heart. Anger. Pain. Humiliation.

Fear.

I drown them all out with a scream. "This is such bullshit!" I tear at the handcuffs again, the chains rattling in mockery. "Tell me what to do, Rage! How can I break out of handcuffs? There's got to be a trick or something!"

"You need to apply enough force to break the chain," Thanatos chimes in, sounding miles away through the speakerphone. "Or slip your hand through. Is your hand small enough?"

I push my thumb as far into my palm as I can and try to squeeze my hand through the cuff, but it catches on bone and merely adds to the bruises already forming. "I could break it," I mutter, looking around the car for something to use. "I saw that in a movie once. They broke their thumb and got free." A chill rushes down my spine and I bite my trembling lip. Looking up at the growing flames, I consider the pain Rebel and Ruin are going through right now.

If I can do this, if I can actually break my hand and free myself, can I still make it in time to save them?

"You will *not* hurt yourself," Rage growls. "Do you hear me? We're almost there. We'll get you out."

I stare at the gun that Rebel left with me. "I have a gun. Maybe I can shoot the chain." I also saw that in a movie, I think. Or was it an axe that Rose used in the movie *Titanic* to cut the handcuffs keeping Jack prisoner while the ship sank?

Would Rebel keep a hand axe in a Lamborghini?

"Just sit tight; we're almost there."

The minutes crawl by as black smoke rises into the night sky. A siren wails in the distance, no doubt heading this way, and all I can do is wait.

For Rage and Thanatos to arrive.

For Rebel or Ruin to reappear from within the flames.

Or for my heart to break when they don't come back.

If Rebel and Ruin don't make it out, what does that mean for me and Rage? Will he still want me if I'm the reason they died?

My thoughts spiral as I picture the long stretch of time ahead of me until my death, an empty void of nothing, nowhere, no one. I press my palm to my stomach and close my eyes, praying that if by some miracle I get pregnant, my baby will still have a loving father in their lives. Images of each brother flicker through my mind, one man after the other rocking a baby in their arms. Up until now, I've been picturing either Rage or Rebel as the father, but this time, Ruin joins the rotation. With a baby of his own and a family to care for, would he finally be comfortable enough not to hide behind a mask?

I picture Ruin standing by an open window with the baby, a soft white curtain billowing around him and obscuring his face. The man's silhouette shifts, growing taller, broader, until the curtain falls to the side to reveal not Ruin—but his eldest half-brother Thanatos, a gentle smile curving across his scarred lips as he looks up to find me standing beside him. In his sharp eyes, I see a piece of them all—the deep obsession from Rage, the calm decisiveness from Ruin, the playful affection from Rebel, and something new from Thanatos himself.

Kindness.

When Rage and Thanatos finally arrive, skidding to a stop beside my car, I'm at a loss for words. I don't want to let any of these men go before realizing whatever future lies ahead for us. The good, the bad, and all the in-betweens.

Thanatos is faster than Rage, jumping from the driver's seat and lunging for me. While he snaps open the passenger door and grabs the handcuffs, I watch as Rage runs inside the burning building and disappears behind a wall of smoke. My heart leaps to my throat, but Thanatos is already shoving a lock inside the keyhole to my cuffs and twisting. The moment they snap off, he pulls me from the vehicle in one swift motion and swings me around until I'm seated on the hood of Rage's SUV.

The metal is warm on my bare thighs, and I look up at Thanatos's face, remnants of my daydream blurring with reality. Dazed, I whisper, "will you take care of the baby?" Tears well in the corners of my eyes, and I hastily brush them away. "I need to know if—if something

happens, that I still have someone—that you could—"
Huffing, I stop myself from continuing. It's foolish to think that Thanatos will want anything to do with me if we don't make it out of this incident unscathed.

His touch is gentle as he lifts my chin, the embers in the air reflecting in his dark eyes. "I promise, Princess, that no matter what happens, I will be there for you and your baby." Rubbing his thumb across the bruises on my wrist, he lifts my hand to his lips and kisses the tender flesh, looking every bit as kind as he did in my daydream.

Maybe it wasn't a dream after all. Maybe it was a glimpse of the future.

My heart aches as I breathe in smoke and fumes. Thanatos is blocking the fire from view, but it's impossible to ignore the inferno growing by the minute. Heat swells around us, but Thanatos makes no sudden movements, keeping his eyes locked on mine. His jaw sets with a firm clench of his teeth, and I get the impression that he doesn't want to stand here with me—but Rage likely ordered him to keep me from running into the burning building after him.

It's a smart call. I'm surprised that he didn't tell Thanatos to drive me home.

But once Rage and Rebel suddenly burst from the front of the building with Ruin's arms thrown over their shoulders, it makes sense. They need a driver to take Ruin to the hospital.

"Get in!" Rage yells, dragging Ruin's unconscious body to the SUV. Thanatos and I both jump into action, helping them lift Ruin into the backseat. While I slip through the back door and lay Ruin's head in my lap, Thanatos and Rage jump into the front while Rebel joins me in the back. We peel out of the road so fast that Rebel and I have to hold Ruin steady so he doesn't slide off the leather seat.

His body is burning hot, his clothes charred or missing altogether. *Shit.* I don't know anything about burns. I don't have any medical experience. I don't know—

"Check for breathing," Thanatos instructs calmly, "then find his pulse. If you see any burns—"

"Take his clothes off," Rage interrupts, "anything restrictive. Belt. Shoes."

Rebel is already in motion, tackling Ruin's belt, then what's left of his shoes, discarding his knife holster and melted boots to the floor. He tears open what's left of his brother's pants while I carefully remove the top half of Ruin's broken mask, my hands shaking.

I lower my ear to his mouth and listen for the rattle of air in his lungs. I double-check that his chest is rising and falling before declaring that he's alive. "He's breathing," I tell everyone, "but it's not good. It's—it's hard to know."

"You're doing great," Rebel says, somehow staying eerily calm. "Check the pulse on his neck."

His heartbeat is slow, but still present, contrasting the race of my own heart.

Rebel squeezes my hand for a quick moment. "Breathe through your mouth, baby, it's easier."

I do as instructed, but nothing prepares me for the

sight of Ruin's body. It's hard to tell which scars are fresh versus which ones are old, the skin blemished across most of his torso and arms. I keep my eyes on his body for fear of looking at his face. He hasn't wanted me to see him without his mask, and it feels disrespectful to look now when he might be...

I swallow hard and sweep my gaze across the red patches of skin on his chest and shoulders, breathing through my mouth to avoid the scent of charred flesh. It's impossible to ignore, but I try as best I can.

"Hey, Ruin," I murmur, brushing his hair from his face. Even that feels damp, either from sweat or gasoline. Chemical fumes pour from his body and sting my eyes, but I tell myself that if he still smells like gasoline, that means the fire didn't touch him as badly as it could have. I guess that's a blessing, if we're counting miracles.

"Take him to The Box," Rage says suddenly, "Wren Sakovia will meet us there."

I glance up and catch Rage's eyes in the rearview mirror. I've heard of The Box—it's a medical facility the bratva uses when they want to avoid hospitals and legal documentation of patient stays. "Surely he needs a hospital," I protest, narrowing my eyes. "With a real burn unit."

"They handled our burns the last time, baby," Rebel says gently, flicking his gaze from his youngest brother's face to mine. "They'll have records of the damage from before and know exactly what to do for him."

"And which spots to treat," Rage adds, his gaze piercing mine. "A burn unit would fuck him up even more. He has dead zones on his body until you cut deep enough to get through the scarring."

"It doesn't look like he'll need skin grafts." Rebel flops back into his seat and starts to run a hand through his hair, then winces and pulls it back in front of him. I finally get a good look at his injuries from the side, finding ash smeared across his face and neck. His hands are bright red, shaking as he twists them in the passing streetlight.

"You're burned," I breathe, choking on guilt. It's my fault that we left the house. If I hadn't been so focused on Sara—

Sara!

I gasp as a knife twists in my gut, regret flowing freely through my veins. Not only did my men get hurt, but we never found Sara. She could still be out there screaming, begging for someone to save her... and just like with Ruin, I'm too late—too weak—to stop any of it.

Clenching my fists, I blink tears from my eyes and vow to do better. To *be* better. If I'm going to protect the people I love, I need more than a secondhand gun and a few self-defense lessons.

I need to learn how to put a bastard down.

No more tears. No more second-guessing. No more relying on others to keep me safe. This life is brutal, and the only way we're all going to make it out alive is by being ruthless.

Someone's hand finds mine and squeezes. My breath catches as I squeeze back, tearing my gaze away from our joined hands to Ruin's face. High cheekbones, clean-shaven jawline, smooth-skinned, white scars along the entire right side, a missing eyebrow, and one eye that's lighter in color than the other, a soft shade of gray.

Breathtakingly beautiful.

He returns my stare with a determined set to his jaw and a fire in his eyes that I can feel in my soul, continuing to squeeze my hand as he works his jaw like he wants to say something.

"Shh," I coo, running my hand over his hair. "Don't speak. Just breathe." Curving my back, I brush my lips over his forehead and press a kiss to his heated skin. "I won't ever let him hurt you again," I vow, my determination setting into place once he grips the side of my shirt with a trembling fist. "I promise."

CHAPTER 2

CELIA

THE BOX IS a bratva medical facility hidden inside of a warehouse on the west side of the city. Not everyone born into the bratva knows about it, but those who actively contribute to the bratva's inner workings—gambling rings, protection fee collection, gun running—always have a reason to pay the sitting medic a visit. Although I've heard stories from my brother, I've never been there before now.

I never imagined I'd have a reason to pay The Box a visit.

Then again, I've never had three mafia boyfriends before.

A medical team rushes to meet us with a gurney the moment we pull up to the curb. As the boys help their brother out of Rage's SUV, I continue holding Ruin's hand, determined not to let go. He squeezes my fingers like a lifeline, his eyes searching for mine every second we're in transport.

One of the medics tries to brush past me. "I'm sorry, ma'am, you're going to have to let go."

My heart hammers loudly in my ears. "I'm only letting go if he does." I loosen my grip, but Ruin's remains strong, pulling me even closer. The entire team rushes through an open dock door and I have to jog to keep up. Despite the building's exterior, the inside is pristine. Concrete floors are professionally treated and spotlessly cleaned, with a straight path leading through rows of partitions separating the cavernous room into smaller pods. Each pod is filled with bright overhead lighting running across the tops of the partitions and with rolling medical equipment and carts. The team ignores all of them and rolls Ruin to one of the larger pods in the back, where a doctor in a surgical gown awaits. Despite the paper mask covering his face and the cap tied around his head, I recognize him immediately.

"Dr. Sakovia." I breathe a sigh of relief. Thank God he's already here. Alongside him is a team of five dressed similarly to him, including the sterile gloves on their hands.

"Put him on the table," Wren instructs. My hand slips free from his while they transfer him, and I'm unable to maneuver back by his side once they start taking his vitals and hooking him up to machines. They peer inside his throat, slip two IVs into his forearms, and begin triage and treatment.

Gently, Rage touches my lower back once the medics begin debriding the burnt flesh from Ruin's body. "You won't want to see this," he murmurs, tugging on my arm. "C'mon, let's get some air."

"I'm staying."

Ruin's eyes finally close as the adrenaline fades and whatever drugs they've given him kick in.

Rage and I stare at Ruin together. "He's in good hands," he murmurs, squeezing my hip. Then he coughs, a wet sound that sends icy panic down my spine.

"Serena, see that both Rebel and Rage are treated for smoke inhalation and other injuries," Dr. Sakovia interrupts, glancing up at us. "You may stay, Miss Monrovia, if you do not interfere. There's a chair over there." He nods toward a metal folding chair sitting against one of the partitions. "But the moment you do, you will be escorted out of the building."

"I'll be fine." I touch Rage's cheek to reassure him. "Go get checked out."

One of the medics, who I assume is Serena, leads Rage out of the room and across the hall where Rebel is already being assessed. He's sitting on a patient cot, staring into the distance with a blank expression. Another shiver wracks my body, and I wrap my arms around my middle. I glance back at Ruin one more time before deciding that Rebel needs some attention, too. Slowly, I cross the short hallway and step into his room.

"Hey," I breathe, slipping into the space between his thighs. "You okay?" Rubbing my hands up the outside of his thighs, I feel the remnants of debris on the coarse denim and pull my hands back to find black and gray ash dusting my hands.

Rebel's gaze focuses, landing on my hands instead of my face. His lips pinch into a frown while he tries to brush them off, and then he sighs and pulls them around his neck. Leaning into my body, he exhales into the curve of my neck and wraps his arms around my waist. "Yeah, baby, I'll be okay."

"Both of you need to remove your clothes," Serena instructs. "Miss Monrovia, please sit over there while they change." She nods towards a matching folding chair to the one in Ruin's room. After a moment, she adds, "Do you also need treatment?" Her eyes are glued to my wrists, and it takes me a moment to remember that I'd been handcuffed. She's likely seeing the bruises.

"She stayed outside," Rebel rumbles, kissing my cheek. "Which I hope she isn't mad at me for."

Shaking my head, I tell him, "it seems silly to be mad about that right now." I step back to allow Rebel to undress, but he snags my fingers and wraps them around the hem of his shirt.

"Help me?"

Carefully, I peel off Rebel's clothes. There's nothing sexy about it—but my stomach churns as I catch fresh burns on his neck, back, and shoulders. Some of his hair has been singed off, and the laces on his Converse have melted. Rebel uses scissors to cut them off, and only once they're in the discard pile do I see that the soles are also melted.

How hot was it inside the building?

Once both men have stripped down, Serena hands them gowns and sets them up with oxygen masks, instructing them not to speak while it's being administered. Both men ignore the straps for their heads and hold the masks up to their faces, all three of us staring across the hallway to where Ruin is being treated. Eventually, one of the medics closes the curtain and blocks him from view.

Rage grumbles, clearly disliking it.

"He'll be fine," Rebel insists, lacing our fingers together. "Wanna sit up here with me, baby?"

I shake my head. "No, I'm okay." The last thing I want to do is sit down. Energy pulses through my body, making it hard to stand still. Not only are my men injured, but Sara is still out there. "Maybe we should call the police."

"They'll already be processing the scene." Rage rubs the back of his neck. "We'll have to see who's on bratva payroll to keep things quiet."

"No, I mean to find Sara." I try to rub off some of the soot from Rebel's hands onto my pajamas. "I have insurance for the boutique." Thinking about the headache that awaits for *that* debacle makes me uneasy, but so does everything right now. In order of priority, fixing my business now seems firmly planted at the bottom of the list. Looking around the room, I frown. "Where's Thanatos?"

Rage removes his oxygen mask to answer. "Likely cleaning up our mess."

"As usual," Rebel snickers. "He's good at it, too."

"What do you mean?"

"When we were kids, he used to come to our conferences at school. You know, the ones when you get into trouble. Our dad couldn't be bothered to care, and our mom wasn't always reliable, so Thanatos handled everything."

I look between the brothers, puzzled. "I thought he wasn't that much older than you." Surely, they didn't allow a teenager to attend meetings for their parents.

Rebel clicks his tongue. "Haven't you seen those grays? He's always looked older than he is. When he was fifteen, he could grow a full beard. He'd pretend to be our dad in all the meetings."

"There were a lot of meetings," Rage muses, "because *someone* sold cigarettes in the bathrooms."

With a grin, Rebel winks. "What can I say? I've always been popular."

Heavy footsteps sound down the concrete hallway, and Thanatos appears. He looks between us and the curtained room, his expression unreadable. "How is Ruin's condition?"

I grip Rebel's hand tighter while Rage slips an arm around my waist. Standing between the two of them gives me strength that I'm not sure I deserve. I'm not the one who walked inside of a burning building and made it out alive. "They didn't say," I answer, pinching my bottom lip between my teeth. "But they sure didn't want me in there."

Thanatos runs a hand through his salt and pepper hair. "That's typical for doctors." He paces the floor in a tight line and repeatedly flips a pocket on his tool belt open and closed with every other step. "I talked to Ezra.

He isn't thrilled about the fire, but he's even less thrilled about our father. It's easy enough to blame faulty wiring for an old building going up in flames, so we're covered on that front, but someone called in *another* fire across town, and they found a body this time." He takes a breath and looks at me. "It's female. No ID yet."

My blood runs cold. *Sara.* What if it's her?

"Oh, God," I moan, nausea creeping in. "Did she—did she burn alive?" I take a quick breath. If Sara dies, I'll already blame myself, but if she dies *horrifically,* I'll never be able to look myself in the eye again.

"We don't know that it's Sara," Thanatos says slowly.

"Is that supposed to make me feel better?" I snap, glaring up at him.

The three brothers share a moment between themselves before Rebel finally says, "well, yeah."

"None of this is your fault." Rage rubs soothing circles into my lower back. "It's our problem, so we're going to fix it."

I shake my head. "It's *our* problem." Meeting each of their eyes one after the other, I make sure they're listening. "We all need to work together on this. No more late night excursions with only two of you at a time. All five of us need to be tracking him down as a team, or we'll never catch him. It's like he's slipping through the sewers or something." I crinkle my nose, *definitely* not liking the sound of that. "But if I'm with you, maybe he'll get closer."

Rage grinds his teeth. "*No.* You aren't taking a single step outside. You're going straight home."

"Back to the cage?" I pull away from him and turn to glare at his stubborn self. "I heard you on the phone, Rage. You wanted me locked up again. *Fuck that.*" Rebel reaches for me, but I smack his hands away. "And *you*, handcuffing me to the car! I swear to God, it's like the two of you think I'm made of glass." Walking over to Thanatos, I grab his arm and pull him into the conversation. "I've been doing well with my training, and if you're so nervous about it, I can stick with Than the entire time. He'll watch over me to make sure I'm safe while you two search another part of the city. And Ruin —" I pause, unsure how he will fit into the picture while injured. Sighing, I shut my eyes. "He needs time to heal."

Thanatos clears his throat but doesn't pull his arm free from mine. "Even injured, Ruin is fantastic with surprise attacks. We need him on standby for when we catch Dad. He can come in for the kill."

"*I'm* gonna kill him," Rebel protests. "He tried to blow Ruin up! *Again!* He came after my girl!" His eyes lock onto me. "There's no way in hell that I'm not gutting the bastard."

"We can *all* claim our pound of flesh," Rage rumbles, "but Celia is *not* getting involved."

"Like hell I'm not! I want my pound, too!" I smack Thanatos's chest. "I'm bulletproof with Thanatos beside me. Besides, I need to make sure Sara is okay. We need to put her under witness protection, or something, while we get rid of your father. Maybe she can stay at the Baranova estate with Valentina for a while."

If Sara is still alive.

I swallow the lump in my throat. "So first things first, we find Sara, get her somewhere safe, work as a team to find your dad, and then we kill him. *Together.*"

Rebel's eyes glitter with excitement. He drops his oxygen mask behind his back and ignores Serena's frown of disapproval. "You're so hot when you're fired up, baby. Come get a kiss."

Rage grabs his shoulder to keep him from getting up. "Sit *down.* We're not going anywhere until we learn more about Ruin's condition." His eyebrows pinch together as he looks across the room to the curtain separating us from his youngest brother. "This should be a family decision since it involves all of us. He needs to be a part of this."

All four of us turn to look at the curtain. We can hear the medical team working just beyond, steadfast and determined to treat Ruin's injuries. I have no idea of the extent of his injuries, but one slow survey of the room quickly proves that it's not just Ruin I have to worry about, it's all of the brothers. They may seem okay on the surface, but not all wounds are visible to the naked eye.

Some run deep, aching in the marrow of our memories and clawing at our souls. When I look at each man in the room, I can catch glimpses of that pain in the tight set of their shoulders, the dull haze clouding their once-bright eyes, the shake of their shallow breaths. They may want to charge ahead to rip their father's life up from the root and throw it into the fire, but they'll be running from one problem directly into the next. Because as much as my men may never want to admit it, they aren't invulnerable.

They're human.

Seeing the damage their father can still wreck on their lives might be a reminder they never wanted... and one I never knew they needed.

CHAPTER 3

REBEL

By the time the doctors are finished treating my brother, hours have passed, and I'm ready for a polar dip in the ocean and a long, cold slumber beneath the waves. Not permanently—but long enough to numb the thoughts running through my head. It's not my body that hurts—it's my heart.

I should have pulled Ruin out of the building before he ever had a chance to get hurt.

As Celia sits by Ruin's bedside with his hand in hers, I watch the two of them together. The steady rise and fall of his chest. The way she gently folds herself over his lap, her eyes slipping closed even after she wills them open again. It won't be long before she falls asleep, but it'll be longer still before Ruin wakes up. I hope that he's elated to find her lying beside him. I would be.

My fingers twitch with the need for a smoke. A joint. Hell, a hit of whatever shit they gave Ruin. But ever since I went on a bender and took a few too many pills, doctors don't like to give me the good stuff. I've been left with some extra strength Tylenol and enough burn cream to lube up my entire body twice over, like that'll be enough, but it'll have to suffice.

Rage is giving me the side-eye, like he expects me to rummage through the locked cabinets in the back for something stronger.

To his credit, I might have a few years ago.

But back then, the point was to numb myself to *everything*, and right now, I don't want to miss a single second of time with Celia or Ruin. I just want to take the edge off so that I can get some sleep. We're in for a long night in The Box, and it isn't exactly what anyone would call comfortable.

Thanatos keeps pacing from one end of the building to the other, like he's on edge, too. He keeps checking his cell phone like it's some kind of lifeline, but I don't know what he's waiting for. News on Sara? Information about our father? A call from our boss Ezra to tell us how fucked we are?

I blow out a breath and fiddle with the cotton blanket in my lap. My burns already hurt, but the pain will double within the next few hours, and I desperately want to be knocked out when they do.

Ruin's going to be in so much pain when he wakes up. I can hear him screaming in my head, the same way he did all those years ago after the first fire. He was only twelve then, but I'm sure he remembers every cursed moment during the blaze and all the seconds of agony soon after. I know that I do.

Especially after pulling him out of an inferno for a second time.

Rage leans against a desk and crosses his arms over his chest. "You good?" he asks, leveling me with one of those *older brother* looks that means I shouldn't bullshit him. He ran into the fire after me and Ruin, receiving the least amount of damage from the blaze, but he's chugging water like his life depends on it. I'm sure he doesn't like the reminder of our past any more than Ruin and I do.

"Thanks for showing up," I tell him. "I mean it. I couldn't have lifted that beam without you." I tried. I even threw all my rings to the floor before wrapping some fabric around the wooden beam and lifting as hard as I could, using every muscle in my body the best I knew how, but it wasn't enough. I wasn't strong enough to pull my brother out from underneath it before Rage arrived.

We could have both died in there tonight.

Man, I need a fucking cigarette.

I tap my fingertips against my thigh. "I should have noticed all the gasoline on the floor sooner. I should have gone in there after him the second he tried to run ahead. But I just—" I clench the blanket in my fists. "I didn't want Celia to go in there." Pinching my bottom lip between my teeth, I try to roll my tongue over my snakebite, but the piercing is missing. I had to take it out shortly after we arrived to The Box. Sighing, I run a hand through my hair, grimacing at how goddamn *crunchy* it is. "I smell like shit," I groan, flopping down on the mattress.

All burnt flesh and sour regret.

Guilt curls on my tongue, and I spit onto the ground. "Fucking hell, man. I can't believe this shit."

"It's not your fault." Rage uncrosses his ankles and comes to sit on the bed next to me. There are two dozen of them lined up into two tight rows in the back of the warehouse, none of them comfy, all of them having seen at least one death in their lifetime. Rage is completely unbothered by this, and I know I should be, too. But I look up at Ruin, hooked up to all of those monitors and tubes, and I can't help but wonder if he'll be another name scratched from the Reaper's list of souls to take.

It's unsettling, and I'm not fucking handling it well.

My stomach churns and bile rises to the back of my throat, hot and disgusting. I jump up from the bed and bend over a nearby trash can, choking on saliva and what little remains of my dinner. Fucking *nasty*.

Rage hands me a water bottle as I slip back onto my bed. We stare at Celia and Ruin, both of them unconscious now, as I sip the cool liquid. "It's not fair, y'know?" I peel the label off the bottle and drop it onto the floor. "We've already been through this bullshit once, and now she has to go through it, too."

"It's better this time," Rage muses, his gaze fixed on the couple in front of us. "Don't you think?"

I crinkle my nose. "There's not a *better*. There just *is*. And what this is, is bullshit."

My older brother grunts and leans back on his cot, resting his back against the cold metal bars making up a headboard. After a moment, he says, "I don't want her out there looking for him."

"If she wants to go, she'll go. Better that she do it with us than alone." I close my eyes and try to picture what it will be like to travel the city with Celia, but all I see are bright red flames licking toward the ceiling of her boutique. I snap my eyes open and take another swig of water. "You can't lock her up again, Rage. She won't forgive you."

He scowls, suddenly looking older. The lines around his mouth crease into deep grooves, and there's a twin row of wrinkles in his forehead. He doesn't like hearing the truth, much less adhering to it. "I know."

I lie down and turn onto my side to look at him. "So what are you going to do?" He's grinding his teeth like he used to do when our father would tear a belt across his back. Funny how you remember the most terrible details in times of crises.

Swallowing hard, he sets his water bottle down on the floor and throws his arms behind his head. I bet he wishes he could escape to the gym right now to lift weights. If we were home, I have no doubt that he would spend hours bleeding out his frustrations on his body, lifting twice the amount of weight than he should just to exhaust himself.

Kind of like how I'd kill for a bottle right now.

"I'm going to sleep," he says finally, turning his frown onto me. "And so should you. We need as much rest as we can get if we're going hunting tomorrow."

I glance over at Celia, expecting her to be alone with

Ruin but finding Thanatos hovering nearby. He drapes a blanket over her shoulders and retreats to another folding chair sitting near a partition wall, apparently settling in for a night of staring. I guess silent contemplation runs in the family, after all.

"What about Sara?" I don't really care to help strangers, but Celia will tear herself apart if it brings her one step closer to finding the college girl. "Did they ID the body yet?"

"Not yet."

"Have the cops called?"

"No, but when they do, I don't want Celia answering." Rage closes his eyes like he's going to sleep sitting up. "We need to keep her as calm as possible, and answering questions from the police about the fire will make that difficult."

"You underestimate her, man."

He takes a deep breath. "I don't want to lose her."

Yeah, neither do I.

If there's one thing I know for certain today, it's that Celia's twin brother Mikhail is an asshole.

The man is a splitting image of her, except for the fine-lined stubble on his jaw and his lack of tits, but everything else is eerily similar. Same skin tone, same hair color, and same piercing hazel eyes. Hell, they're even the same height, coming to about five foot eight or nine. That, and he can be just as stubborn as she can.

"What do you mean, I can't see her? She's my *sister*! Who the hell is she to you?"

Thanatos is running bouncer at the door to The Box, refusing him entry. I'm sure it's not just on Celia's behalf, but all of ours. We all slept like shit and could use another few hours of rest before greeting the world.

Mikhail Monrovia either didn't get that memo, or he doesn't care.

"I'm her protection detail," Thanatos replies, squaring up to the smaller man. "And you won't see her unless she approves it."

"You work for me!" Mikhail's grin is sharp. "Stand down, Riot."

There's that name again—the one Than programmed into Celia's phone contacts beside his real name.

I quirk an eyebrow. "Since when did he decide to be cool like us and get a new name?"

Rage chuckles. "Remember what he was wearing when he worked for Katya?"

Rolling my eyes, I chuff. "There's no fucking way he picked that name because of that stupid gear he wears." Then again, he's never been the most creative. "There's *no* way."

Footsteps shuffle behind us, and Celia slides in beside my brother and me. "What's going on?" Loose strands of hair stick to her cheek, and I brush them back with a smile.

"Morning, sleepyhead. You were out like the dead."

She throws a halfhearted glare my way. "Not funny, Rebel."

I wrap my arm around her waist and pull her into my side, pressing a quick kiss to the corner of her lips. "I thought it was pretty funny."

"Seriously, who's yelling? Because they're gonna wake Ruin up—" Her eyes widen as she spots her brother beyond Than's—*Riot's*—broad shoulders. She gasps and slips from my arms to greet him.

Great.

Rage and I follow closely, neither of us keen on having her deal with her asshole brother alone, but it quickly turns out that she doesn't need us.

"What the *hell* do you think you're doing?" She hisses, grabbing his wrist in a vice grip and hauling him toward the front door. "This is a medical facility! People are resting!"

My heartbeat trills with pride. Yeah, that's *my* girl.

Mikhail steps outside with her, but so do my brothers and I. We form a wall of muscle behind her, the three of us ready to jump in at a moment's notice.

"What are *you* doing?" Mikhail asks, gesturing towards us. "I find out that your shop burnt down, and then you're not even home! The police have put out an APB for you, Celia, and our mother is about to tear down the city looking for you!"

Celia winces. "I'll call her."

"Oh, really? Like you've called me over the past few weeks?"

"Cool it!" She shoves his chest. "I love you, Mikhail, but you did a shitty fucking thing, and you know it!"

He shakes his head. "What would you have had me do? Let that fucker take my wife? Let all his constituents get away with it? I'll burn the city to the ground to keep her safe. You *know* that, and you know that I'd do the same for you!" He turns the heat onto us. "So what the fuck are you doing with these guys?"

Celia looks at the three of us, her expression softening. "They're mine, Mikhail, the same way that Valentina is yours."

It takes Mikhail a second to process this, and then he's not glaring nearly as hard. "I need a drink," he says finally, engulfing his sister in a hug. "And I think we need to talk."

I clap my hands together and grin. "Count me in for that drink."

Rage smacks my shoulder before he remembers that I'm injured. I hiss, and he quickly mutters an apology. "No drinks, but we can talk."

Mikhail releases Celia and nods. "We can head back to the estate if you guys are discharged."

"We're not," Celia says quickly, "we have to stay. Ruin's still inside." She loops her arm through her brother's and walks him toward us. "But you can order us some breakfast as an apology for the rude awakening." Her cheeks flush a pretty pink and she clears her throat. "Mikhail, you've already met Rage. This is his brother Rebel, and that's Thanatos. They're my—" She takes a quick breath and smiles the sweetest damn smile I've ever seen. "They're my family now. So be nice."

"Family?" Mikhail's face pinches. "What, did you get hitched, or something?" He inspects Celia's left hand for a wedding band and frowns at the bruising on her wrist from the handcuffs last night.

Oops.

"Not yet," I chime in, "but by the time the baby comes, you bet your ass, she will be."

"*Baby?*"

Celia's blush deepens. "Maybe we should, ah, have that drink after all."

This time, it's Thanatos who grumbles his agreement. "I think I need a whole damn bottle to get through today."

CHAPTER 4

RAGE

MIKHAIL MONROVIA IS the type of man who pushes buttons. Not just the tiny ones that light up sky rise elevators like Christmas trees—but the big, red buttons encased in glass and surrounded by warning signs that read *DO NOT PUSH!* He slams his fist on those huge buttons with a maniacal grin on his face, all because he wants to see the chaos that follows.

My brother Rebel is much the same way, pushing over dominos to watch the crash.

I don't like having them in a room together for this exact reason, but with Celia in our lives, I have a gut feeling that it's something I'm going to have to get used to. While Mikhail absentmindedly flicks a switchblade in his hand throughout our entire conversation, Rebel tracks the movement with this tiny smile on his lips, like he's tempted to kick the knife out of Mikhail's hands to see what the man will do if Rebel reaches across the table and claims it for himself.

I stomp my heel on Rebel's toes and grind down, but it's no use—he's strung out from the lack of sleep and the crash after an adrenaline rush, both making him distracted. He's hardly paying attention as Thanatos draws a circle on a paper map of the city, pinpointing our father's most likely location based upon the body drops over the past few weeks and the abandoned buildings in the vicinity. There are only so many places he can hide.

In fact, I'm anticipating that the reason we haven't sniffed him out yet is because he's been on the move since reentering the city. After spending the past few years on the run, I doubt he can sit still.

Much like Rebel.

My annoyance grows—*quickly*—until Celia suddenly twines Rebel's fingers in hers and leans into his side, curling beneath his arm as he drapes it over her shoulder. He settles down in an instant, damn near purring like a cat, the smile curving on his lips softening as he presses a tender kiss to Celia's temple.

I'm not jealous. I'm *not*.

I drum my fingertips against my thigh as I fight the wave of envy pulsing through my veins. Celia and I have made progress—but not like that. Not *nearly* like that. I need to be patient. I told Celia that she could fall for my brothers first—and I meant every word. I still do.

But that doesn't make it any easier to witness the two of them falling harder with each passing day.

Celia lifts her tired gaze to mine and smiles, making my heart *thump* hard inside my chest. Not only is she beautiful, but she's observant, reading both me and

Rebel with such ease that I wouldn't have noticed if she hadn't given me a hint.

That smile speaks volumes, and it soothes the jealousy burning inside my heart.

I don't need to be jealous of my brothers. When Celia finally comes to me of her own volition—of her own *heart*—she'll fall just as hard for me as she has for the others.

She *has* to.

Mikhail claps his hands together once he and Thanatos have hatched a plan for taking down our father. I've listened intently up until the last minute, missing the most vital part of the conversation...

Like, how the fuck we're going to take him down once we've found him? Who will make the kill—and who will ensure he suffers for every fucked-up thing he's done not only to our family, but to every woman he's carved up for fun. I grind my teeth as I picture it—the moment my father meets the Reaper. Part of me believes that it should be Ruin to make the final cut, but another part of me longs to be the one to cave in his skull with my fists. Rebel likely won't care to take the kill so long as he gets in enough hits to burn off his anger from Celia's attempted abduction.

I watch Celia for any sign of hesitation or remorse, grateful when I find none. Her eyes are tired but clear, with her resolve as strong as ours.

I always knew I picked the right woman to love.

Mikhail raps his knuckles on the table to collect everyone's attention. "Alright, let's get this shit show on the road. One less murdering lunatic in town will be good for everyone. I'll sleep better at night knowing that he can't reach my sister, seeing as she keeps such... *interesting* company." The insult slides right off my shoulders. I don't give a fuck what Mikhail Monrovia thinks of me —regardless of his status as my future brother-in-law. He can go fuck himself with his disapproval.

Locking eyes with his sister from across the table, Mikhail adds, "you should stay here until we've eliminated the threat, Celia."

Her back straightens as she bristles. "No. No way, Mikhail. He's after *me*. If he finds out that I'm here—" Celia glances at the partition blocking Ruin's unconscious body from view—"he'll come for more than just me." Quieter, she adds, "I'm not the only person whose blood he wants. So I'm going with you. I want to find him just as much as you do."

I stare at my beautiful, stubborn woman, two emotions crashing against each other like waves inside of my heart. Pride swells like a fever, but on its heels is heavy dread churning inside my gut. If we split Ruin and Celia up and secure them in different locations, my father will have to choose a target... which means only one of them will be vulnerable to attack at a time.

Celia is willing to risk her life if it means keeping Ruin safe.

What she doesn't seem to understand is that it will never come to that—I won't let either of them die. We aren't splitting up anymore. We're seeing this through to the end—all of us, together.

Clicking his tongue in clear disapproval, Mikhail stabs the sharp tip of his switchblade into the table. "That's exactly why you should stay here. He won't get into The Box, Celia, even if he figures out where you are. If by some heinous miracle he does—which I *sincerely* doubt—with another target so close, he'll have to choose one of you to go after. He can't kill you both."

Rebel snorts. "Uhh, did you miss the blazing fucking inferno back at the shop?" He flicks crusty, burnt hair from his eyes, frowning as it falls back over his forehead. Hastily brushing it away, he huffs, "he'll set fire to the whole goddamn city if he thinks it'll help lure her out, especially if he thinks he can take Ruin out at the same time. He'll want to make them both suffer."

Mikhail isn't convinced. "That's exactly why he *won't* light another fire. That was a message, not a murder attempt."

"Sure fooled me," Rebel murmurs moodily.

I stare at Celia to gauge her mood, but she stares stonily ahead, glaring at her brother, undeterred in the slightest. "I'm not going to sit here while everyone I love combs the city for this bastard. I'm coming, too. That's final."

My heart trills with love for this woman, and despite how bone-tired I am, my cock threatens to rise. I clench my fists and clear my throat. "She'll be safe with us." I meet her gaze and nod. I'm not keen on the idea of her running through the city in general, but for the first time in my life, I'm even less fond of locking her down. If she's standing still, Dad could track her just as easily as we do, and if he's been paying attention, which I'm sure he has, he'll suspect that we're in The Box if any of us were injured from the latest arson.

He could be hiding around the corner as we speak, waiting for the perfect opening to slither through.

"We can't move Ruin," Thanatos says slowly, staring into the distance. "It's too risky with his current condition."

Before Mikhail can open his big mouth, I growl out, "*Don't* suggest we leave him behind."

A muscle in Mikhail's jaw twitches. "He's a liability at best and a death sentence at worst."

"He's a goddamn soldier," I hiss, slamming my fist on the table. "Out of everyone here, he's the one who takes the worst hits and keeps fucking going, because that's what he does best. He keeps on living despite every painful breath it fucking takes." Anger makes my blood pressure rise, and I lace my fingers together to keep from bashing my knuckles against Mikhail's pretty face. "We are *not* leaving him here with a target the size of Texas on his back."

"Ruin comes with us," Celia agrees, looking between me and Mikhail. There's a spark of determination in her eyes that sends a rush of pride through me all over again. "He's got more motive to kill the man than any of us sitting here."

Rebel rouses himself enough to chime in. "Fucking right, he's coming with us." Pressing a kiss to Celia's cheek, he smirks and whispers something in her ear to make her blush. I kick his shin, and he grins, tossing me a wink.

Cheeky bastard.

Without warning, Thanatos stands from his seat and bolts around the table towards the hallway. I jump up and pull out my gun, expecting to find my father's cruel smile taunting me from across the room. The longer we sit here, the closer he undoubtedly gets. It's only a matter of time before he finds us, and then—

"Ruin!" Celia gasps, both she and Rebel jumping to their feet as my youngest brother shuffles across the concrete floor in an attempt to make it to the table. He's rolling two IV poles in front of him, his back arched and his breathing shallow as he leans on them for support. Thanatos reaches him first, looping Ruin's arm over his shoulders to hold him up. Rebel takes his other arm while Celia slips between them both, damn near crashing into his chest. At first, she hovers there without touching him, her hands frozen in midair. Then Ruin dips ever so slightly, folding his body over hers in a gradual collapse. If it weren't for my brothers holding him up, I have no doubt that Ruin would engulf her like a wave crashing over the shore as it gives into the pull of gravity.

All of my brothers are quickly giving into Celia's magnetism, even *Thanatos*, in his own way. It's an inevitability for us and always has been, really. But instead of fighting that pull, Celia is finally learning to accept it. To *embrace* it, just like she's trying to do with Ruin right now. She carefully wraps her arms around Ruin's torso and allows him to fall into her at his own pace, the two of them sharing a moment unlike any I've ever seen. For once, Rebel isn't twitching with impatience for the next step; he's joining them in the embrace, hooking his arm over Celia's hips and sliding into place beside them.

Thanatos is the one who doesn't move, stiff as a board as he watches their display of affection. Conflict wars in his eyes until Celia reaches out her hand and grabs the hem of his shirt, pulling him closer. He doesn't hug any of them but takes a deep, full-bodied breath and places his open palm on Celia's lower back.

A part of me is jealous that Celia ran to Ruin so quickly, but if there's one thing I'll never begrudge her, it's loving my brothers as much as I do.

More than I do.

Slowly, I tear my gaze away from the tender scene unfolding and tap my fingertips on the table to draw Mikhail's attention. "Like I said." I don't bother hiding my smirk. "Ruin is coming with us."

CHAPTER 5

RUIN

THE FIRST THING I feel when I wake up is the heat. Sometimes, when my body fully remembers itself—every ligament, every tendon, every millimeter of skin and muscle and bone—that's all I feel. The memory of the flames licking across my skin. I know it isn't real, because my body hasn't fully been mine since that night twelve years ago.

Part of it belongs to me, but the fire stole the rest.

This time, however, the throbbing heat has a pulse. Every thick layer of flesh on my body burns with unmistakable heat, the topmost layers of skin having melted away to reveal the wet flesh underneath, my blood boiling and turning to steam, clouding my vision so that all I see is a red haze and all I taste is charred flesh. I crack through the plate of rust covering my eyes and blink up at a starless sky, knowing that even if the fire is out, I'm still burning on the inside.

A part of me will always be burning.

Voices float through the air, obscuring the erratic beat of a heart monitor, O2 sensors, and every other wire connecting me to life. The doctors and nurses in the room watch with bated breath as I pull at the cords, a few of them helping disconnect me, while a few others ensure that I keep the most important needles and tubes embedded in my skin.

I don't much care for them, can barely feel the tug inside my veins and the pull on my skin, but on some level, I understand the necessity.

What am I without a body to ground me to the earth?

I still need answers to questions I cannot ask, so for now, I relent.

But that doesn't mean I stop moving.

Her face is like a beacon in the darkness, calling me closer. I can hear voices—all familiar—but there's only one I truly listen for as I shuffle from one room to the next, the weight of my muscles finally settling onto the bones, making it harder and harder to move as the drugs the doctors have given pump through my system.

I'm not supposed to be awake—but I am.

I'm not supposed to be *alive*—and yet.

She's standing in front of me, her eyes glistening with unshed tears and her gentle hands hovering on the precipice of touch. My body aches for more than the pain, and suddenly, it's as though I'm falling, falling, falling—into her open arms.

Everything hurts, but this—the press of her lips on my forehead, the ghost of her breath across my bare cheek, the way her soul stares into mine—somehow, *this* hurts a little less.

I think I might be ready for *a little less* and then, maybe, *a little more*, too.

In time.

Celia takes a breath, her bronze eyes shimmering like pennies in the rain. "You shouldn't be up yet." She slips her hand in mine and leads me to one of the beds lined up in neat rows like narrow coffins, unaware that the only thing I see in The Box is Death, and the only thing I hear are its rattled moans whispering secrets about the other side. I don't tell her this, because I don't want her to hear them, too.

The voices of the damned begging for scraps of our lives.

Sometimes, I wonder if I'm the only one who hears them, or if we're all pretending as we look the other way and paint smiles on our faces.

But the smile Celia gives me isn't one of feigned pity or grief—it's relief, overwhelming as she gently coaxes me into lying down and slips onto the mattress with me, careful not to tangle inside my double-IVs. My body is covered in gauze and tape from head to toe, but Celia rests her cheek on my chest anyway, listening to the beat of my heart in the exact way I want to listen to hers.

"Sleep with me, Ruin," she murmurs, closing her eyes. "Just for a little while."

Slowly, I lift my fingers to her hair and weave them through the silky strands, knowing that I'm dirtying her, understanding that I'm ruining her, but unable to help it.

She might be ruining me, too.

I exhale a breath I didn't realize I was holding, and the pain eases from my limbs as I drift away into the darkness of slumber, guided by the gentle glow of Celia's light as she keeps the whispers of Death at bay.

I sleep, and for once, I dream.

Not of screams, or heat, or pain.

But of the parts of my body that have long been missing finally returning home, lured by the subtle glow of a once-weeping soul nestling next to mine.

Neither the police nor the bratva have found the college girl. I overhear my brothers discussing the details while Celia sleeps soundly beside me. Sitting up pulls at my bandages, but I do it anyway, knowing that stretching my body's limits is part of the healing process. I'm not burned nearly as badly as I was thirteen years ago, so in theory, I should heal much faster. Even if I don't, I can't lie here forever.

No matter how tempting the woman beside me.

I reach around the mattress and find the hidden tear in the side, slipping my fingers through the slit to pull out a rolled-up bag of pot from when I was last here. Rebel perks up at the sight, quickly coming over to help me roll a blunt and share in the spoils. He has to step outside to light up, but once he's back, I can see the tension slipping from his shoulders as he exhales a cloud of smoke. I do the same after he hands me the blunt, inhaling as deeply as I can and holding it until my lungs burn.

The nurses disapprove, with the bravest of them scowling at us from across the room as she rolls away oxygen canisters, but none of them try to stop us. They know we've been through hell more than once, and one little game of *puff, puff, pass* isn't going to kill us.

Celia stirs from her slumber, cracking her eyes open to peer up at us through the smoke. Once her mind catches up to what she's smelling, she chuffs, running a hand through her tangled hair and down her face. "Unbelievable."

Rebel kneels on the edge of the bed and leans over me to grin at her. "Want a hit?"

She crinkles her nose. "No thank you."

Exhaling in her face, he steals a kiss and hums against her lips. "It'll help with the stress."

"I'm not stressed."

"Mmmhm." Rebel kisses her cheek before returning to his side of the bed. It's a tight fit with the three of us, so he slips onto the cot beside ours. "We're getting ready to roll out. Mikhail said something about a trip to the police station."

Celia looks over to the table with only Thanatos and Rage still present. "He's good at that kind of thing." She waves her hand in the air. "Smoothing things over. Talking to people." Quieter, she adds, "Maybe they've found Sara."

I share a look with Rebel, both of us unsure of the best way to respond. The marijuana is a little stale but working wonders, and it loosens my tongue. "Maybe there is nothing to find." My voice scratches my throat, and I have to clear it. I take another hit before passing the blunt to Rebel. "It's a good thing, *krosotka*. She is better off being dead."

Wringing the thin bedsheet in her hands, Celia shakes her head. "You're wrong. There's so much to live for."

"Maybe. Maybe not." I run my palm over Celia's soft thighs. *This* might be something to live for. I wonder if Sara has that—something to hold on to through the pain of life.

Clearly, my father does.

I wish he didn't.

Rage wanders over while Thanatos walks the long stretch of hallway and through the front door, stepping into the morning sunlight without a single moment's hesitation. Unlike him, leaving the cool, dark comfort of The Box is going to hurt me. I close my eyes and breathe through my nose, knowing that my last seconds of comfort are in this moment. The subtle warmth of Celia's body, the weight of her against my side, the drugs pumping through my system.

I can hear the medical team preparing to-go kits for us, mine undoubtedly being the largest. One of them clears her throat and wanders closer, the patter of her footsteps like falling rain on the sidewalk. "Excuse me, Miss Monrovia?"

The soft click of Celia's throat as she swallows precedes her voice. "Yes?"

"Could you come with me for a moment? I'd like to show you the contents of each medical kit and how to use them. Our patients don't always follow instructions once they leave, especially when it comes to their after-care—" There's a flinty edge to her voice, like she's speaking from experience. "And these boys in particular like to skip steps."

Ah, so she is.

I don't remember her name, but she must remember ours to keep up with our charts and medical history. Briefly, I wonder what they say about us. Negligent with wound care, orders too many refills, misses his checkups —the possibilities are endless, really, when you consider how anal Rage is about protocol and how lax Rebel is with procedure. It's almost enough to make me smile.

But what *really* works is the feel of Celia's lips gently pressing a kiss to my scarred cheek. My chapped lips quirk up into a crooked smile. She spares me a quick glance and smile of her own before slipping away to follow the nurse across the room, and all three of us watch her go. I press my fingertips to my cheek, expecting the tingle from her touch to disappear. I'm grateful when it doesn't.

"You're blushing," Rebel teases, pointing what's left of the blunt at my face. "Damn, bro, she's got you *good.*" He snickers and stubs the roach against his cargo pants. Both of my brothers have dressed, neither of them in their usual attire, leaving me the odd man out wrapped in little else than gauze and tape.

Rage stares intently at me. "How are you feeling?"

It takes me a moment to piece together the right words. "Like I'm floating." I stare at Celia as she sifts through the contents of each of our medical packs. I'm not sure if it's the medicine or the pot or the woman standing in front of me, but for at least this one moment, I'm okay.

Maybe better than okay.

I take a deep breath, awaiting the tightness inside my lungs, for the moment the pain burrows deep and latches onto my organs, but whatever feeling persists is a dull ache rather than a roar. I can live with that.

"Are you sure?" Rage narrows his eyes as he scans my body. I know he's not looking for injuries on the outside —he's trying to glimpse what could be hidden within. Trauma exists in more than the physical plane—its scars the brain, too.

But as long as I don't *think* about—

I cut off the violent crackle of flames inside my head with the sound of Celia's voice, listening intently as she asks the medic questions. "I'm fine," I tell Rage, knowing that he won't believe me but saying it anyway. I have to be fine, or he won't let me leave The Box. Thankfully, however, Rage's need to win against our father makes quick work of any hesitation he has.

Admitting that I'm hurt means that Dad won. Pretending that I'm fine—that *all of us* are fine—is how we take our next steps... away from the flames... and toward the woman holding the brightest possible future for our family in her hands.

Chapter 6

Celia

THE CAR RIDE back to the club is quiet. Rebel drums his fingertips on his knees, then the armrest, then the back of the driver's seat, and everywhere else he touches, while Thanatos drives us home on back roads. The club is in full swing when we arrive, so he pulls the car around to the back and cuts the engine. None of us move.

I squeeze Ruin's hand until he squeezes back. "Ready?"

He grunts noncommittally, and one by one, we peel ourselves off the leather seats to help him up the stairs and through the back door. While Thanatos scans the area and nods toward the two armed guards standing watch, I follow the remaining three brothers inside. Rather than take the grand staircase to the second floor, Rebel leads us to a hidden service elevator in the back hallway. Once inside, Rebel loops his arm over my shoulders and presses a kiss to the top of my head.

As I take a deep breath in, I smell the remnants of smoke in our hair and clothes. It fills the elevator like the start of a bad dream, and when I close my eyes, flames flicker into the night sky.

Ruin takes a sharp breath, his body stiffening in front of me.

"Almost there." Rage keeps his arm wrapped around his younger brother's waist, holding him steady as the elevator comes to a stop.

"I'm fine," Ruin mutters, stepping into the hallway as soon as the doors slide open. "Let's go."

Before I can follow them into the apartment, Thanatos grabs my wrist and pulls me to a stop. "We need to take a detour."

My heart skips a beat. He couldn't possibly want to train *now*, could he? One glance at my pajamas makes me wince. They're silky but skimpy, leaving little room for strenuous movement without showing off the curve of my ass or an ample eyeful of cleavage.

If Thanatos gets me alone, I'm not sure what to expect. Will he be the kind man who breaks me free from handcuffs and apologizes for dropping a vase at my feet, or will he be the force of nature throwing me to the mat and panting in my ear?

Rebel pulls a face as I slip from beneath his arm. "Man, what now? Can't it wait?" He scratches the top of his head, ruffling his dirty locks. "We've all had a shit night and an even shittier day. Let it rest, man."

Thanatos narrows his eyes. "You know who isn't resting?" A muscle in his jaw tics as he tightens his grip on my wrist. "Our psychopath father. I need her for a minute. Go take your fucking shower."

I place my hand on Rebel's chest and pop up onto my tiptoes to press a quick kiss to his lips. "Go on. I'll meet you inside in a minute."

He glowers at Thanatos before stealing a deeper kiss, cupping my face in his hands as he sighs against my lips. "I want you naked the minute you step inside the house, okay? I want to wash your hair."

Rolling my eyes, I pat his chest. "Okay, tough guy." I bite my lip as I meet Ruin's gaze, then Rage's beside him. "Will you guys be okay?"

"I've got him," Rage assures me, nodding. "We'll get him settled in."

"I'll be waiting," Ruin murmurs, his wide eyes peering into my soul. An electric tingle rolls down my spine at the intensity of his gaze. The warm glow from the hallway light turns the scars on his cheek a deep orange, but the white bandages trailing down his neck and chest glow like the flames I thought we'd left behind.

I still don't know where the two of us stand. His obsession with knives—with finding my soul—with the way his fingers dip between my thighs—all feel distant when I barely recognize the man standing in front of me. I know that despite the drastic change in his appearance without the mask, nothing has really changed between us. It's still Ruin staring at me, like he always does.

But something feels different this time, and it has nothing to do with the scars etched into his body.

"I'll be there soon," I promise, giving him a small smile. "I promise."

Thanatos tugs my arm, finally pulling me free from their gravity.

Walking away from the boys to follow Thanatos feels like a fever dream. In another reality, after everything we've been through, I'm sure that it's the last thing I would ever do. But in *this* life, I'm thrust into a kind of chaos that I can't wish away. Thanatos understands that chaos on a level I can't fathom, so following him across the hall feels like the next step in understanding the darkness pervading these men's lives... the first step having long since passed unawares.

When did my journey begin? Was it the moment I accepted my invitation to *Midnight* and gave my body away for a moment's reprieve from the pain of unending heartbreak? Or was it when Rage first saw me at the Baranova wedding and suddenly decided that I was his new favorite obsession?

I stretch my fingers and swallow hard, the memory of Rage's throat in my hands burning in the depths of my mind. I squeezed as hard as I could, and the man smiled at me before passing out. That could have been the moment I unwittingly sealed my fate to these men—by taking a piece of their darkness and claiming it as my own.

In the end, where the journey began doesn't matter.

It's how the journey ends that's important.

I won't let another arrogant piece of shit determine my fate, no matter whose father he claims to be. From what the brothers have told me, he wasn't much of a father at all. Just a sperm donor who stuck around way longer than was welcome.

Thanatos unlocks an unmarked door on the same hallway as the brothers' apartment. Recessed lighting outlines the perimeter of the room and reveals a single panel of chain-link fence directly in front of us, sectioning off the entryway from the rest of the room. Behind a locked gate lies dozens and dozens of weapons ranging from serrated hunting knives to metal baseball bats and gleaming handguns, all neatly organized, with ammo boxes and larger rifles and shotguns stacked waist-high on the floor.

"I should have known you'd have an armory," I murmur, quickly memorizing the code Thanatos puts into the electric lock. He scans his palm, too, just like the brothers do for all the other doors on the second floor. The lock *clicks* open, and he swings the gate wide enough for me to step through. I nod toward the chain-link fence. "Someone could easily cut that."

Grunting, Thanatos grabs a pair of gloves sitting on top of an open box of ammo, puts them on, and closes the gate behind us. Once it clicks into place, a low hum fills the room with a buzzing sound, and the hairs on my arms stand on end. He reaches out and grabs the fence, and a spark of electricity *zaps* his gloved fingers. Lifting an eyebrow at me, he releases the metal fence then shucks the gloves, tossing them onto a cardboard box.

"It's electrified," he explains after a moment. "If

someone tries to cut the fence, they'll get one hell of a jolt."

"You could have said that instead of putting on a show." Rolling my eyes, I shoulder past him toward the weapons on display. I haven't the faintest idea which one I should grab—or if we're here not just for me, but for all of us. "Does everyone have a favorite?" I eye the knives, wondering if they've all been used before. They gleam in the light, looking sharp and dangerous as hell. Each one has a leather sheath strapped to its side.

I can't imagine wearing one of those on my belt.

Glancing at the guns, I bite my bottom lip. Hell, I can't imagine wearing one of *those*, either. Shuffling toward the baseball bats, I notice that a few of them are dented and worn, and a heavy metal crowbar lays discarded on the silver counter beneath them. A dried, flaky brown substance has chipped off, dusting the metal surface like rust. I try to keep a poker face.

I *really* don't want to know what happened.

"Those are Rebel's." Thanatos comes up behind me and pulls one of the most worn bats from the wall. He swings it underhanded toward his elbow, making a *whooshing* sound as it whirls through the air. "This one's seen a lot of damage. It's unbalanced. Heavier at the top." As he places the bat back onto the prongs along the wall, I try not to picture it swinging into someone's temple and bashing their skull in.

I fail miserably.

Shivering, I wrap my arms around my middle. "I didn't think he was a fighter." Maybe that's stupid of me, but out of the four of them, he seems the most like a lover.

Thanatos meets my eyes. There's no pity or annoyance, only truth. "We all are, Princess. We have to be, or we won't survive." He grabs a knife and places it in my palm. "I've taught you the basics of unarmed self-defense. We need to practice what to do when you have a weapon. Let's start with knives, and then we'll move up to guns."

"Aren't guns more practical?"

"They're faster," he admits, looking away from me to stare at a wall of pistols. "But if you miss, you're fucked. A knife is more intimate than a gun and harder to knock out of your hand. After seeing what my dad's doing to the other girls—" His teeth clench. "Let's just say, he won't want to make this a clean death. Guns are pretty clean overall. Knives aren't. Bats and other blunt objects are the best for prolonging a victim's pain, but he doesn't have the stamina for them, and none of the victims showed signs of blunt force trauma. They were all carved first, then burned."

My stomach churns. "That's—that's what he wants to do to me?"

Exhaling slowly, Thanatos sinks lower as his shoulders slump. He leans closer to me, refilling his lungs the same moment I do. The echoes of smoke and flame overwhelm my senses, starting with the grit on my teeth and quickly advancing to the unexpected heat burning my lungs. He draws a breath as he wraps his hands around mine, closing my fingers over the handle of the knife. "I don't know what he wants to do with you, Celia, but I know it won't be pretty. If he gets a hold of you, it's going to hurt. A lot." Pulling my hands closer to his body, he aims the sharp edge of the knife at a soft spot on his side. The serration catches on his t-shirt and tears a small hole in the fabric. "You need to gut him before he can hurt you. Right here," he says, holding the knife to his body, "or here."

As Thanatos shows me every weak spot on the male body, I pay close attention to remember every detail. It's not just my life at stake—but Ruin's, too. And although Rage may claim that Ruin is a fighter, he's clearly hurting from his injuries.

What I fear the most aren't the burns, though—it's the damage hidden underneath.

"What was it like the last time Ruin was burned?"

The question catches Thanatos off guard, and the tip of the knife slips against his abdomen. The t-shirt cuts like butter, but so does his skin. A thin line of red appears instantly, welling with blood. He doesn't react other than to frown at the cut.

I pull the knife away and quickly apologize. "I'm so sorry! I didn't mean to—"

"It's alright." Lifting his shirt, he presses the hemline to the wound to stem the blood flow. "You don't have to push hard to make someone bleed, so remember to *really* go in with intent to hurt someone, or it'll only be a surface wound. See?" He lifts his shirt higher for me to see the cut. "It's barely bleeding."

A bead of sweat rolls down his abs, disappearing into

the waistline of his black cargo pants. I've seen Thanatos half naked a dozen times now, if you count tank tops and gym shorts as partially nude, but the way his brow crinkles as he stares down at the injury, quickly followed with his heavy gray eyes flicking up to mine beneath those long lashes, makes my body heat in a way that it really, *really* shouldn't.

I quickly move to put the knife back into place on the wall, only for Thanatos to grab my hand to stop me. He guides the knife back to his body and wipes the blade on his shirt to clean it. "Never put a dirty weapon back on the rack."

My throat clicks on a swallow as his shirt rides up, revealing the flat plane of his muscles underneath. *Damn it.* What is *wrong* with me? Why can't I notice something other than how warm his skin is through his shirt or how firmly he grips my fingers in his? "That doesn't seem very sanitary," I murmur, completely and utterly *lame* in my response. Who worries about how sanitary cutting someone is when you're learning to kill?

He grabs a clear bottle of liquid on the counter beside him and squeezes a few drops onto his t-shirt. As intense alcohol stings my nose, he continues to "clean" the blade with his shirt, only succeeding in cutting a strip clear off the bottom. He doesn't seem to care, too focused on his task.

I can see where Rage gets his cleanliness habits from.

Once the knife is shining again, he releases my hand and lets me put it back into place on the rack. "Try out a few different sized knives to see which you like most.

Consider your grip—how well can you hold it? Try moving your arms and body to get a feel for each stroke. Use some of the moves we've practiced during our lessons."

My brain melts with each new thing he says. He's staring right at me—studying my reaction or, heaven forbid, gauging how well my body moves under his direction. It's the same thing we do on the sparring mat, except the stakes are higher and the space much smaller.

I pick up a different hunting knife while Thanatos's voice echoes in my head.

A knife is more intimate than a gun.

Unbidden desire rolls through my body like a steady fever, making me sweat. All of a sudden, it's like I'm sitting on the bathroom counter all over again while Ruin pries my thighs apart to play with my pussy.

With his knife.

As Thanatos rambles on about proper weapon usage, I fight the embers of need blooming deep inside my belly. I've seen Ruin's dick in the morning sunrise inside my bedroom—it's veiny on top, with a red blush that extends from the narrow tip halfway down his shaft. A slight curve up towards his stomach makes me wonder what it would feel like inside of me—as hard and unforgiving as the handle he slipped past my lips, or would it be as soft and shy as his kisses, building slowly into a toe-curling crescendo—

"Are you alright?"

Thanatos presses his calloused palm to my forehead, hovering way too close for me *not* to smell him. The usual scent of sea salt and clean linen from his morning shower have long since been replaced with the musk that only men can produce—a heady, full-bodied scent that touches something primal inside of me, and I barely manage to choke back a needy moan.

His onyx eyes bore into mine, widening the moment my lips part.

Shit, did I just moan out loud?

He inhales calmly, *way too damn calmly*, and trails his fingertips from my forehead down to my cheekbone. "You feel flushed."

My skin tingles from his touch while my heartbeat kicks into overdrive. "I'm—I'm fine. Just the, uh, fire. I got a little burned. Not, like, *hurt*. But like a sunburn." For some reason, I think that pulling my pajama top to the side to show him my flushed neck and shoulder is the key to diverting his attention away from the fact that not only is my body on fire, but my panties are suddenly *soaked*.

I hastily clear my throat. "See? Just a sunburn."

His fingers travel lower, ghosting across my jawline on their way to my collarbone. Pressing his thumb against it, he swipes a perfect stripe across my heated skin, all the way to the tip of my shoulder. Licking his lips, he hums deep in his chest. "I see."

Fuck.

It feels wrong to picture both Ruin and Thanatos naked in the same breath, but all of a sudden, not only is Ruin kneeling between my thighs without his mask on, but Thanatos's body is hovering over mine, his back bent so that he can lower his lips to the very spot his fingers now touch.

But when I refocus my attention and flick my gaze back up to his face, his lips aren't ghosting across my shoulder like they were in my mind—they're hovering a mere inch from *my* lips.

I jump back so fast that I stumble, gasping as I blindly reach out for something to hold on to. I trip over a metal ammo box on the floor and fall backwards in my haste to put some distance between me and Thanatos.

He's quick to react, snatching me from the air before I manage to grab onto—*oh yeah*—the fucking electrified fence. As he spins us around, we tumble against the weapon rack, his breath hot and heavy on my neck as he shoves my back into the wall of guns. Clenching his eyes shut, he shudders from head to toe and growls in the back of his throat. "Learn how your body reacts—"

The hard length of his cock presses against my stomach, a reminder of how strongly his body affects mine. The silver flash of heat in his eyes as he snaps them open is new, though, as is the tight clench of his jaw.

He's not reminding me of our very first lesson together—he's reminding *himself*.

"—and control it," we say in unison, our breaths mingling in the air.

"Exactly." Slowly peeling his body from mine, he sighs. "*Control.*" Once he's safely retreated a few more feet away, he buries his hands in his pockets and stares at the weapons over my head.

Shit. This isn't good.

It's one thing for him to have to master his own body —but it's another if mine is reacting to him, too. We can't *both* be tempted. It's a disaster waiting to happen. A horrible, terrible thing that can never, ever, *ever* become reality. I feel like a shitty person for even being tempted in the first place.

Grimacing, I tell myself that it's because he looks so much like his brothers. That's it. They all look alike, and I'm attracted to Rage, Rebel, *and* Ruin, so it makes sense that I could be attracted to their older brother, too. It's genetic, or biological, or whatever. Pheromones. Hormones. Tricky, little bastards that get humans in trouble.

Or knocked up.

The air punches from my lungs.

If I couldn't get knocked up by three boyfriends, maybe *four*—

I clench my fists hard enough for my manicure to cut into my palms. *No.* No way. I'm not going down that path. It's selfish and cruel and manipulative to use someone for their sperm. I want a baby—a family—and I'll get one *without* sleeping with the older brother as an insurance policy, thank you very much.

The whole idea feels even more absurd once I realize Thanatos won't even look at me. He gestures vaguely to the wall of hunting knives without making eye contact. "Grab a few to take with you. We'll start practicing with them."

"Great," I murmur under my breath. "Can't wait."

If I'm expecting a reply, I don't get one. Instead, he

mechanically unlocks the gate, then the exit, and walks me across the hall to the apartment. Once I've stepped inside, he wastes no time in releasing the door so that it slams shut behind me.

He didn't even bother saying goodbye.

I hate how much that hurts.

CHAPTER 7

THANATOS

EVER SINCE I WAS YOUNG, I've made a point *not* to want things. If you don't want something, you won't be disappointed when you can't have it. Celia feels like one of those desires I've spent my whole life pushing away.

She should be inconsequential. A blip on my radar and nothing more.

But as soon as she was locked safely inside my brothers' apartment, I went back to the weapons locker and breathed in her lingering scent in the air. After the kind of night we had, there's little of her left beneath the smoke and salt, but if I close my eyes, I can taste her sweet perfume and pretend that she's still here with me.

Touching me.

With a groan, I cup my erection and squeeze, knowing exactly where this is going. It's the same routine I've had for the past week. Every time I get close to her, I feel like I'm a fire hydrant about to explode. The pressure builds to a breaking point until finally, I can't take it anymore.

I *have* to relieve the tension or I'll go insane.

Pushing a button hidden beneath the counter, I activate the security monitors linked to the club's surveillance system. As the screens hum to life, I check for the only ones I'm interested in—anything with a glimpse of Celia. The videos and pictures downloaded on my phone are of a woman I recognize but don't actually know: a past version of Celia that's only a part of who she is today. The 4K feed in front of me, however, shows the woman who's captured my attention as much as she's captured my brothers'.

I shouldn't want her.

The warmth of her touch shouldn't spark a fire in my blood, one that spreads to the depths of my twisted core and feeds off of the distinct *lack* I've nurtured for years. A lack of affection, or intimacy, or desire. For years, I've kept my distance from people, my sole purpose being to destroy the man who ruined my family's chances at a happy future—one that isn't broken and full of bloodshed. Until Celia came along, I hadn't touched a woman in longer than I can remember.

Now, she's the only person I crave.

More than my father, even, I'm ashamed to admit. I'd just as sooner cut ties with the whole investigation and murder plot if it meant I could steal her away and drown in her laughter, her anger, her tears. Every time I picture her standing in front of me, it's never one version of her but multitudes, shifting faster than I can follow. One moment, she's a young woman about to walk down the aisle in a white lace gown, then the next, she's curled in on herself beneath the willow tree in her backyard, sobbing into the grass as the branches blow like a curtain hiding her misery from the world. The images of her spin round and round, between moments caught in suspended laughter at a public event, to the private whispers she once shared with her ex-husband, or her brother, or her friend Lilith.

All of them are a part of her, and I want to gather each and every shattered piece until she feels whole again in my arms.

It's selfish and stupid and completely fucking unforgivable.

Because if *I'm* the one to put her back together, what pieces are left for my brothers?

I grit my teeth as I jerk the tail end of my belt through the loop and unsnap the buckle. If I can't have her, then at least I can have *this*—the scraps that I've stolen from under their noses. This room wasn't meant to have access to more than the club's lower level security feed, but I rigged it to reach every corner of the upper floors, too. There's a camera in each of my brother's bedrooms, their living room; hell, even the *bathrooms*. Rage was thorough with its installation, and it feels foolish to waste technology.

I might as well use it.

Rage greets her in the living room, barely listening to her speak before he tosses the hunting knives in her hands to the floor and lifts her into his arms, carrying her bridal style into his bedroom. He sets her down on her feet and begins undressing her from head to toe, peeling off her clothes and kissing each new inch of skin revealed.

That could have been me ten minutes ago.

While my brother lifts her again and transports her into his shower, I tug my pants below my hips, letting them clatter to the floor from the weight of my weapons' holsters. I don't give a damn about them when Celia is naked right in front of me, her skin still flushed from our encounter in this very room. I breathe in deep and imagine that I can smell her desire, feel the weight of her body on mine as I shove my boxers out of the way to grip my cock, pretending that the heat of my palm is hers instead.

The steam in Rage's bathroom obscures some of the image, but I watch closely through the glass shower wall as he steps in behind her. Rather than touch her, he reaches over her head for a bottle of body wash, lathers his hands, and begins caressing her body.

Someone else steps into the room with a grumbled shout, and I watch as a naked Rebel forces himself inside the shower with the two of them, quickly taking up the space at Celia's backside. He grabs a different bottle and squeezes soap into his hands, then scrubs Celia's scalp.

This isn't what I wanted to see.

With a hiss, I grip my shaft hard, willing my erection to subside, but it's no use. I glance at the weapons on the wall, noting the few that were knocked askew when I shoved Celia against them, and one deep breath is all it takes for me to refocus on what could have been, right here in this very room.

Instead of my brothers spreading kisses down her spine and over her hips, it could have been me. I listen to the steady drum of water hitting the tile floor and imagine that I'm in there with them, breathing in as much steam, washing away the nightmare of the past twenty-four hours.

Celia's voice fills the room as she moans, a high-pitched whine that nestles deep in my groin. My balls ache with a need for release, and I refocus on the monitor. With a few quick keystrokes and mouse clicks, I zoom in and enhance the image, getting a clear view of Rage kneeling between Celia's thighs, with one of her legs draped over his shoulder to spread her wide open for him. She clutches the back of his head while hers falls back onto Rebel's shoulder, and our middle brother is quick to devour her mouth.

Bitter jealousy roars to life inside my heart. Growling, I thrust harder into my palm, knowing that the sub-par friction is nothing compared to the smooth silk of Celia's skin—or better yet, the golden honey dripping down her thighs. I imagine how molten her core is and how easily it would be to slide inside, to lose myself in the bliss of her body. Were I a different man, I might take it for myself without any thought to her own desires, but I'm not a monster.

I'm just a man unable to deny his baser impulses.

They work together to get her off, and then Rage slots himself between her thighs and slams home, making her cries echo throughout the room as he buries himself deep inside of her. Rebel seems fine with taking the brunt of her weight as they lift her off the floor, leaving her at their complete mercy.

Or lack thereof.

Rage pounds into her pussy with a vengeance that fills the air with the wet slap of their skin, his hands holding her hips in place, while Rebel busies himself with her breasts, her neck, the hollow of her throat and all the dirty things he moans into her ear.

I can hear them too, and *fuck*, if it doesn't spur me on.

"You're so wet for us, baby," he breathes, slipping a hand over her stomach to reach for her clit. She gasps once he finds it, her body convulsing as both men teach her new heights to pleasure. Her moans turn into repeated cries that *zing* down my spine and directly into my balls, drawing them up as my release edges closer.

She isn't wet for them, I tell myself. *She's wet for me.*

Her wide, hazel eyes dilated beautifully once I had her pinned against the rack, my erection undeniable between us. During our training sessions, I've played with different positions—drawing my knee up between her thighs to grind my shaft against her ass, or flipping her onto her back just to watch her writhe and struggle beneath me, the feel of her hot breath on my neck as she fights to break free, panting and groaning and making me so fucking hard for her.

I could cut glass with my fucking dick every time I toss her around.

The first burst of my release is proof that I'm no saint. It jets out in a weak dribble that is quickly overcome by wave after wave of sticky cum, overflowing across my knuckles as I pump harder, faster, painting the brushed silver countertop in thick, pearly streaks.

As I cinch my forefinger and thumb beneath the tip and draw out every single drop, regret washes over me.

She deserves every ounce of my cum inside her womb.

I collapse onto the rubber mat on the floor and wipe the cum coating my hand onto my pant leg, grimacing as I notice a stream of white drip down the edge of the counter and onto the floor. I listen to every breath, every moan, every word shared between Celia, Rage, and Rebel, and wonder how they do it.

How do they share someone so completely without losing their minds? How do they know who is her favorite—or do they even care? If she spends the night in Rage's bed, do the others not long for the weight of her head on their pillows instead? Or will they merge these little moments of their lives until they're sharing *everything*—not just the woman, but showers like this one, and breakfasts and dinners and dates in the city, evenings spent lounging on the sofa or wrapped in each other's arms.

Is that what it means to be devoted to someone so completely that you'll sacrifice independence just to be with them? To make them happy?

The three of them exit the shower and dry each other off. Rebel towels Celia's hair dry while she gently pats

Rage's back dry, then both Rage and Celia turn around to help Rebel replace his soiled bandages with new ones.

I shift my attention to an adjacent monitor, the one inside Ruin's bedroom. Although his room is normally dark, this time he's left the light on. He's sitting up in an unmade bed and lifting a joint to his lips, staring at the blank wall with a faraway look in his eyes as he breathes in deep, then exhales a thick cloud of smoke. Beside him, a thick chain is strung across the ceiling, with dozens of different types and sizes of rope draped over it, each one with various knots and ties looped through them. A closet door sits open with clothes overflowing into a messy pile trailing from the floor to the bed, and the bathroom door beside it bleeds dim light into the room. There's little else—no pictures on the walls or memorabilia on bookshelves. There aren't any shelves at all.

Does he feel the same as I do? Left out of the festivities happening just below his feet? Or does he not crave the same attachments that I do?

I lie down on my back and throw my arm across my eyes, listening to the muted chatter between Celia and my brothers, wondering what's on Ruin's troubled mind, and wishing that things were different.

"What did Thanatos want?" Rebel asks, his voice louder now that he's standing closer to the microphone.

"He gave her knives," Rage rumbles.

"*Kinky.*"

"It's not like that," Celia says quickly. I open my eyes and watch as she slips on one of Rage's collared shirts and buttons the front. She fiddles with them, avoiding my brothers' gazes. I sit up and narrow my eyes at the image, humming a chord in the back of my throat.

It *is* like that, though, if the cum drying on my thigh means anything.

She's lying to them.

"He says I need more training."

"You'll have to learn by experience." Rage leans against the doorjamb and crosses his arms over his bare chest. Both he and Rebel are completely naked still, contrasting Celia as she pulls a pair of Rage's boxers up her thighs. "Where are you going, *krosotka*?"

"To see Ruin," she answers simply, slipping past him to enter the living room. "I can't believe you let him go upstairs."

"It's his safe space. He'll be fine for one night." Rebel follows her to the staircase that leads up to the third floor. The only rooms up there are Ruin's bedroom and bathroom, taking up what was meant to be a bonus room when the apartment was first built. No one goes up there except for Ruin.

I glance at our youngest brother on the other monitor, but he still hasn't moved. He's zoned out, big time, but it's probably for the best. Once the meds wear off, he'll be relying on Percocet and pot to fight off his demons.

I don't think Celia should be there when they arrive.

Clearly, Rage and Rebel are on the same page. They intercept her from going upstairs, with Rage being the one to lift her over his shoulder and carry her back to his bedroom. His voice fades as he moves from one room to the next. "Give him some time to process. We'll check on him in a few hours." He drops Celia onto the mattress and crawls onto the bed beside her. Rebel quickly takes the other side, the two of them locking her between their bodies, just like they did in the shower.

"You promise?" she asks, focusing on Rage.

He kisses her wrist. "I promise."

I watch as they all settle beneath the sheets, but as the minutes pass, I catch all three of them tossing and turning. Rebel's the only one lying still, but I have a feeling that's on account of his own injuries, not because he's asleep. His foot bounces as he taps his feet, finally settling once Celia rolls over and wraps her arms around his waist. Then Rage does the same, spooning her from behind and burying his face in her hair.

Ruin keeps staring at the wall, then at the ceiling once he eventually lies down. But I have a feeling he doesn't sleep—not even for a second.

After cleaning up my mess and wiping more rubbing alcohol over everything it touched, I slip inside the apartment, make a pit stop to wash my hands in the half bath, and walk over to the Ruin's staircase. Climbing to the top, I press my back to the door and slide down until I'm sitting on the top step. It's uncomfortable, but I'm sure he's faring much worse. "I'm here, Ruin." I rap my knuckles against the bottom of the door. "Get some sleep."

He doesn't respond. I don't even know if he heard me, and even if he did, I doubt it will make a difference. He slept with Celia in The Box while the rest of us kept watch. There, with all four of us rallying around him, he was safe to dream.

But *here*, locked upstairs in the dark, he's alone again.

Just like he was when hellfire rained down over him.

"I'm right here," I say again, listening for movement through the door. I know he's a grown ass man and that he doesn't need a babysitter, but I mentally prepare myself for a night on watch, anyway.

If anything, it helps keep *my* demons at bay.

Because if there's one way that I've failed my brothers, it's that I let our father get to them. I let him hurt them again, after I'd vowed never to let it happen after the last time.

If anyone is undeserving of their love, of *Celia's*, it's me.

The true fuck-up of the family.

Pretending otherwise will only hurt us all.

Chapter 8

Celia

Luring a serial killer out of hiding is a multi-step process. Part one: pretend that everything in my life is normal. The trouble is, my new normal involves a lot more men than just one hanging around me, and the thought of returning to my clients to assure them that everything is on track for the upcoming charity gala—when absolutely *nothing* is on schedule—feels like the biggest lie of my life.

"I can't do this," I whisper, halting in front of Heather Hanson's ornate front door. My reflection in the intricate glass design is as distorted as this sudden shift back to my old reality feels. "This isn't even the original concept design I showed her. It's a completely different gown!" I shift the box in my arms and try not to let my frustration show on my face. I'm a woman who prides herself in doing good work—the *best* work—and bringing a client a different dress than the one she's expecting raises a huge red flag for both my business and my reputation. "It would be one thing if I had called her ahead of time—"

Rage reaches around me to push the doorbell. "You wanted to help. This is helping."

"I don't see how parading around the city accomplishes anything—"

The front door opens wide a moment later, and Heather looks just as surprised to see me as I knew she would. "Celia, darling, we don't have an appointment until next week." Once she spots the pale blue ribbon perfectly wrapped around the white box in my hand, however, her lips pucker as she attempts not to smile. "It seems you've brought me a gift." Her crystal blue eyes glitter with excitement. Everyone knows that when Celia Monrovia wraps something in ribbon, it's special. "Is that what I think it is?"

I put on a winning smile. "Why don't you open it and find out? Could we come in?"

"Of course. I'll never say no to a gift." Heather stares longingly at the package before opening the front door and beckoning us inside. "You even brought your little boyfriend with you. How cute. Joining her for work today, hm? I bet he's the kind of man who loves to see his woman in action." She winks over her shoulder before leading us into a sitting room. "Now, let's see that dress!"

I've barely extended my arms before she's snatching the box from my grasp. Tugging at the ribbon, she unknots the bow and lets it fall to the floor before popping open the lid. "Oh, it's marvelous! I can already tell." She grasps the fabric and pulls the dress free.

"This is a mock-up," I carefully inform her. "I went with different colors than we discussed, but I know how much you enjoy standing out." The bright gold and maroon sequins sewn into the bodice sparkle in the light, and Heather brushes her fingertips over them as she scrutinizes the design. "If we replace the sequins with beading or faux gemstones, we could further elevate the design, but I wanted your input before moving forward."

Heather holds the dress up to her body and swings her hips. "It *is* different than the initial concept, but you know me well enough to know that I need to be the center of attention. I won't have Janette Fowler outdoing *me*. Last I heard, she was going to wear a feather boa like one of those dancer girls from the twenties. It's casino night, not a speakeasy, for Christ's sake!" She rolls her eyes. "Let me try this on, and we'll see where all the pins need to be. You're ready for that, aren't you?" Not waiting for my answer, she points to the other side of the room. "The lighting is best over there by the window, so you can set up while I get changed."

Once Heather disappears into a back room, Rage checks in with the team through our communications system. Each one of us has an earpiece with a dual speaker and microphone, some kind of state-of-the-art tech that the brothers assure me is not only untraceable but necessary for our operation. "Any movement?"

"No, but we laid the breadcrumbs, so all he has to do is follow." Thanatos's voice is as clear as if he were standing right beside me. I fiddle with the earpiece in my left ear, earning a disapproving look from Rage. It's only inconspicuous if we act natural, but there's nothing natural about having four men whispering in your ear all at once. Then there's the matter of the so-called breadcrumbs the boys laid out for their dad to follow. They've taken over the boutique's social media accounts and posted not only about the fire and the devastation it's laid on the business, but they've left hints about my schedule for the next few days, leading up to the charity gala in a few weeks. The boutique might be gone, but the business lives on.

"It might be a good thing you don't have a storefront anymore," Rebel muses through our comms. "He can't lay any more traps. He'll *have* to come out and grab you."

"How comforting." I smile as Heather reappears with a floor-length mirror in hand. Once she sets it up and gets into position, I quickly get to work pinning all the sections on her dress that will need brought in and hemmed. While my fingers move, the boys continue their discussion in my ear, choosing which clients to visit next and where to have lunch in the city. They debate over which location would be best: a sunlit patio where anyone can easily find me, or a dimly lit dive bar more suited to sneak attacks from serial killers trying to kidnap you.

"I invited your mother to lunch," Rage says suddenly, catching me off guard. "We should go somewhere she might like."

I prick my finger with a pin. "You *what*?" Dread churns in my gut. I haven't spoken to my mother since our phone call a few weeks ago when she found out I was dating again. At the time, I hadn't considered Rage or his any of his brothers as more than a semi-casual fling, but a lot has changed since then. My mother can sniff out feelings like a bloodhound. She'll sense how deep I'm in immediately, and then the questions will start.

How long have you been dating? You're not getting any younger, Celia; are you finally going to give me grandchildren with this fine gentleman?

I try not to snort as I picture my mother's face once she meets Rage. She'll also be able to sniff out that he's a bratva man, and I'm not sure whether or not she'll be happy about it. On the one hand, she'll be glad to fold me back into bratva social life to maintain her own status and reputation, *especially* if I'm going to have children. Heirs are what keep the bratva going—and they're as much bargaining chips as they are cogs in the wheel to keep the bratva going. Alliances are made from arranged marriages and ties to other bratva, and the Monrovia name entering the gene pool won't go unnoticed. I have no doubt that Russian elders have already been talking about my brother since he finally settled down and married Valentina with Ezra and Andrei. With both Baranova and Monrovia blood in its veins, their baby will be heir to *everything* in Harlin Heights, even if it ends up being Andrei or Ezra's child. Their bloodlines are strong because they've *made* them strong.

I'm not so sure that everyone will agree on my child

having such strong parentage, given not only my father's history, but my own track record within the bratva and the brothers' violent reputation. Unlike Mikhail, I haven't exactly made a name for myself. If my mother sticks to tradition, she'll no doubt mention Rage, Rebel, and Ruin's bratva ranks, too. So on the other hand, although she'll be happy with my return to the bratva, she may not be overjoyed about with whom I'm returning.

Rage smiles broadly, clearly on another page than me about the whole "Meeting the Parents" scenario. I don't think he realizes the interrogation we're about to walk into. His brothers, on the other hand, have mixed feedback. They chat in my ear, talking over each other as Rebel says *it's not fair* and Ruin suggests going somewhere private for our lunch date. Thanatos, thankfully, doesn't have much to say other than *hurry up* to keep on-schedule.

Heather catches the look on my face and chuckles warmly. "Has he not met the family yet?" She peers down at me as I mark the perfect hemline for the heels she's wearing. "Better warn him, dear. Your mother's a viper." Meeting Rage's reflection in the mirror, Heather *tuts*. "Adella's got one mean bite when it comes to her children. Watch yourself around her, or she'll snap."

Exhaling heavily, I stand up to check my progress. I don't like commenting on my mother's behavior, so I merely reply, "she just wants what's best for us."

"All good mothers do." Heather admires her reflection for a moment before pulling at her skin to mirror giving herself a face lift. "Whether they *know* what's best is, well, a little harder to parse. My mother, for instance, always said that I should marry for money instead of love, and look how that turned out. Can't stand the man." She runs her hands down her sides and pinches her waist. " But he sure does have a lot of money to burn." After a moment, she smiles wickedly. "Add those rubies you mentioned, Celia, and we can even replace some of these sequins with diamonds. Is there a gold stone?" She spins in a slow circle before turning to face me. "I want to look like I've been dipped in gold so fine that even my husband remembers what a trophy he's bought."

With a promise that I'll deliver on every request, she's satisfied enough to change back into her day clothes and walk us to the door. "Oh, and Celia?" Grasping my hand, she meets my eyes. "I'm so glad you're alright. I heard about what happened to your boutique, and I just—" Shaking her head, she sighs. "The news says that a few women have gone missing. Can you believe it? And Nancy's niece, the one who goes to that community college across the river? Well, she says that all the girls have started walking in groups on account of a rumor about these two upperclassmen kidnapping a freshman after she humiliated them in public. I'm sure it's not that serious," she adds quickly, her mouth curving into a frown. "But it makes you wonder what the world's coming to, doesn't it?" She glances over my shoulder at Rage. "Keep her safe, now. She's a special one."

The warmth of Rage's hand on my lower back eases

some of the tension in my shoulders. His answer comes smoothly. "We will."

"Damn right," Rebel clicks in my ear.

Ruin grunts in agreement, while Thanatos murmurs one little word that makes my heart flutter.

Always.

CHAPTER 9

RAGE

TAKING Celia's mother out to lunch wasn't part of the original plan. Celia and I were supposed to meet with her gala clients today, spend a few evening hours unwinding with my brothers at her house, and end the day with a nightclub appearance—the two of us on stage while Celia sits on my lap in the skimpiest lingerie possible, her hot lips on my ear while I finger her cunt beneath a spotlight. The goal is exposure—use Celia as bait to lure out our father. When people see us together at the club, word of mouth will spread like wildfire. Secrets are meant to be kept at *Midnight,* but I'm not stupid. I know that people talk.

Especially when there's a gorgeous woman on display.

But when Celia's phone rang a half dozen times this morning, all of which being from her mother, I improvised.

Mrs. Monrovia was *not* happy when I picked up the phone, much like I wasn't happy with her tone.

Like Heather Hanson said, the bitch can be venomous when it comes to her children, and the news about Celia's boutique going up in flames didn't go over well with her.

But...

Imagine how lethal she could be when it comes to her *grand*children.

By the time Celia and I arrive at the French cafe Adella Monrovia favors, it's bustling with activity as mother and daughter duos and groups of women purchase dainty sandwiches or pastries to go with their tea and coffee. The lunch crowd doesn't pay much attention to Celia on her own, but the moment I lace our fingers together and bring her knuckles to my lips for a kiss, it doesn't take long for the whispers to begin.

They're not used to men like me stepping into their establishment.

A few of the women, I recognize, chief of whom being Mrs. Monrovia herself. All of the bratva women have laid claim to the far side of the cafe, taking up every single window seat in existence. The thing with bratva women is that appearances matter to them. It's important for others to see who they are dining with, what connections are being made between family lines, and which ones may cross over into business relations—usually, all of them.

In essence, the women's emphasis on appearances is the opposite of what their men need. The *pakhan* is the exception since he's the face of the bratva, but the rest of us slithering through the underbelly of the city take more clandestine measures with our meetings and operations. I'm not used to having business lunches in broad daylight—I'm used to dragging some sorry sack of shit into a back alley and talking with my fists.

This is different, but different might be good for me.

Rebel's voice cuts through our comms unit. "Don't fuck this up."

Noted.

Celia walks in her mother's direction on instinct, hardly looking in the elder woman's direction before her feet begin moving. She cuts across the dining room like she owns the place, not sparing a second glance at any of the other diners. In her eyes, there's only one woman in the room.

One glance at Adella tells me that the feeling is mutual.

I pull out Celia's chair and push it back in for her before taking my own seat at her side, to Adella's right.

A chainsaw couldn't cut through the tension in the air.

"Mom, this is Rage."

Adella doesn't spare me a glance. "When were you going to tell me that you returned home, Celia? I've only been throwing Russian men into your path for the past six months. The least you could do is tell your mother that you're not interested in her choice of men. Not because you're still sad, but because you're *seeing* some-one." She sniffs as she unwraps her cloth napkin and places it in her lap. "I could have spared myself the indignity of telling all of those bachelors that my daughter was still grieving."

Celia's lips press into a firm line. "You didn't tell them that."

After a server delivers a bowl of lemons for our table, Adella replies, "No, I didn't."

This turn of conversation is interesting, and not at all what I'd expected. Celia hasn't exactly said much about her relationship with her mother, so it was easy to guess that they weren't close. I'm not sure why—most bratva women stick together like they're glued at the hip—so animosity between Celia and her mother is a puzzle I have yet to solve.

Rebel comments on the conversation in our ears, and I catch Celia's flinch. "What is there for her to grieve?" he asks, scoffing.

Although I couldn't agree more, unlike my brother, I understand that Mrs. Monrovia won't see it that way. A loss of a husband to death is one thing—but losing him to divorce? It tarnishes a bratva woman's reputation, regardless of Celia's ex-husband's status as a normal citizen and not a bratva member.

Celia has been fighting an uphill battle with bratva tradition and societal expectation since she turned eighteen, if not even earlier. *Sixteen*, maybe, with how early girls are betrothed.

Not my daughter, I silently vow, clenching my fist under the table. *Fuck* an arranged marriage. I won't have my future child become a bargaining chip for some fat fuck to use as leverage for a grab at Baranova bratva power.

If Mikhail has any balls, he won't stand for it, either. Not for his future niece *or* nephew.

I lift my other hand from beneath the table and take Celia's hand in mine, carefully wrapping her fingers in mine and setting them on the table in a public display.

It's more than affection—it's *claim.* I rub my thumb across Celia's ring finger, my mouth twitching at the subtle frown pinching Adella's lips.

"I assure you, Mrs. Monrovia, Celia has nothing to grieve. I'm taking care of her better than her ex-husband ever did." I lick my teeth, enjoying the way Celia's cheeks dust with a rosy pink. "In fact, we're expecting."

Celia plants her heel on my toes and presses down, stabbing my foot as best she can in her little white shoes. "We are *trying,*" she clarifies, her smile tight. "Not expecting."

"We're expecting results," I continue, smiling fondly. "I invited you here today to give you the good news first."

Adella's lips twist into an ugly sneer before she catches herself. Smoothing her expression, she slices a croissant in half before setting it back down on her bread plate without taking a bite. "Good news?" Scoffing, she folds her hands together at the furthest edge of the table. "You are unmarried. You cannot have a baby out of wedlock."

"That's not your decision to make." Celia's grasp on my fingers tightens. "I'm going to have a baby, Mamá, and Rage will be its father."

My heart soars to new heights, filling me to the brim with such warmth and light that even Adella's disdainful glare can't bring me down. I lean over and press a kiss to Celia's hair, enjoying the way she *glows*. Fucking radiant. The little white dress, although not a sundress in the winter, hugs her body in the softest material, like the warmest blanket I've ever known. Her cheeks flush a perfect shade of pink as she meets her mother's eyes.

I can't help but add, "I'll be the first, then my brother Rebel will likely be next. He's trying really hard to beat me, though."

Celia slams her knee against my thigh, bumping the table and clattering the silverware. "He's joking," she says quickly, her voice pinched.

Smirking, I lay my arm across the back of my chair. These lunches might actually be fun. "I wish I were."

"You have *got* to be joking," Adella hisses, glaring at the table next to us that's clearly eavesdropping. "*Two* men, Celia? Oh, your father must be rolling in his grave. Our daughter! A common whore." She shakes her head. "If I'd known that Ted's infidelity would bother you so much, I would have paid him to keep it secret. First the divorce, now *this*."

Celia's gone completely still, her face paling. "What did you just say? You *knew* he was cheating?"

Unbothered, Adella rolls her eyes. "All men cheat, *docha*. Even him." She nods towards me. "I'm sure after you've given birth to your first, he'll wander. Oh, yes, they always do. It won't be long before he finds another hole to fill. Your father didn't even wait until you and

your brother were born; he strayed from our bed before I
even knew I was pregnant." She wrings her hands
together, the first nervous tic I've seen. "But he was my
husband, and we have a duty to our husbands, Celia.
This man—" she points a sharp fingernail in my direction—"is *not* your husband. He'll surely leave you just as
soon as Ted did, especially if you can't produce an heir.
What did Dr. Sakovia say when you last saw him? *Hostile
womb?*" She tuts. "I doubt having two dicks between
your thighs will change that."

Fury roars like a hurricane in my ears, igniting my
blood with a vengeance. It pulses through my body like
lava, thick and scalding hot, tearing a burning path to my
heart. How *dare* this woman speak to my wife that way.
Mother or not—and *clearly* not a good one—she doesn't
get to speak to Celia that way.

I stand from my chair, my throat burning with every
despicable thing I want to say to this woman. Celia grabs
my wrist and tugs hard, but she's no match for my
strength. I glare at Adella Monrovia with every ounce of
my rage, baring my teeth at her and hoping she cowers.

To my surprise, she doesn't look the least bit intimidated. She clearly knows who I am—and what I've done
to lesser humans—and yet she doesn't bat an eye as I
tower over her. From this height, Adella has clearly aged
well. I can barely see the wrinkles around her eyes, and
there's not a speck of gray in her hair. But her eyes—
those dark, fathomless pits of righteous *shit*—are as
ancient as the night sky. She looks *tired,* worn out from a
life running circles around a man who may not have

loved her and two children who took unconventional paths to find love.

Thanatos's voice is loud and clear in my ear. "Tell me when."

A tiny red dot appears on Adella's chest, both women freezing as they realize what it's from. Adella looks at the laser dot, then up at me, then through the wide window to wherever she thinks my older brother is hiding. "You'd shoot a defenseless old woman?" Shaking her head, she chuckles as her shoulders relax. Fearful at first, but only for a moment. When she realizes that whoever is aiming a gun at her chest is with us, all the fear in her eyes melts away. "You can't shoot me without consequences. Do you really want to explain to the *pakhan* why you killed an elder—your future child's own flesh and blood—after he's only just let your beast of a brother back into the bratva?" She clicks her tongue. "He'll kill all four of you in a heartbeat. There's no room for bad blood in our ranks." Lifting an eyebrow, she continues, "oh, yes, I know who Thanatos is. I also know who *you* are, clearly more than my daughter, or she would never have gotten close to you. Do you know what he's done, *docha*? What *all* of them have done? They're unworthy of you, of your blood, and will sully our good name if you breed with them."

Breed with them.

I nearly laugh at loud, but Celia finally moves, slowly standing from her seat. Whipping her hand out, she *cracks* her mother across the cheek, slapping her hard enough that Adella's earring pops off. It tumbles forgotten to the floor, but no diamond can compare to the way my woman *burns.*

An inferno rages in her eyes, making her body shake from the raw power coursing through her veins. "You've said enough."

The red dot moves to Adella's forehead, right between her eyes, as she turns her head to face her daughter. She doesn't speak, which gives Celia the floor.

"You have preached about my precious reputation since I was a little girl!" She straightens her spine and glares down her nose at her mother. "After Dad died, you told me that he'd picked out a husband for me—oh yes, I haven't forgotten that monumentous birthday present —*a forty-year-old man.* It's no wonder I ran away from the bratva and its fucked-up traditions and into the arms of the first man I found! Ted! A man *you* approved of, if you recall!"

"I wanted you to be happy. He seemed to make you happy."

"He was all I'd ever known!"

Adella's lips pinch into a frown. "Sit *down*, Celia."

Our altercation has drawn the attention of the room, leaving little room for other conversation. Every bratva woman's ears are burning from how closely they're listening, and all of the regular city inhabitants are all looking the other way while pretending not to listen. I'd rather have them carefully observe, like the Russians. At least they're honest with their curiosity.

Celia flicks soft waves of her chestnut hair over her shoulder. "I know you think that my broken marriage is my fault—that somehow, you've failed as a mother for producing a daughter that can't have children—but I'm here to tell you that none of it is my fault, and you shouldn't automatically blame me for everything that's wrong in your life. Dad cheated, then he died, and now you're bitter and alone since I won't call you. None of that is my fault. I wouldn't even say that Dad's faults are *your* fault. But this—" she gestures between the two of them—"*this* is entirely your fault. I wanted you to be happy for me. I wanted you to think, *Celia has found someone that makes her happy!* Let's celebrate the miracle of life and love and try to patch our relationship. If not for our sake, then for my unborn child's." Tears fill the corners of Celia's eyes, but none fall. "I may not be pregnant yet, but I won't stop until I have a child to love. Maybe it will have my genes, maybe it won't, but the one thing I now know for *sure* it won't have?" She draws a deep breath, her shoulders dropping as some of her anger cracks. "A grandmother."

In the raw silence that follows, I wrap my arm around Celia's waist and pull her into my side. Grinning wickedly at Adella, I say what's on my goddamn mind. "The next time my wife's name leaves your lips, make sure that you have nothing but good things to say, or I'll rip your fucking tongue out myself." Steering Celia away from the table, we walk through the silent dining room and out the front door, leaving the bitch for good.

I don't give a damn if Adella Monrovia falls to her knees and grovels for forgiveness—not on my fucking life will I let her near my woman, or our child, again. I had hoped, perhaps foolishly, that having a strong bratva woman in our corner would be a good thing. Another mama lion to protect her family should be an asset. But nothing about that woman screams *important cargo.*

Heather was right—Adella is pure venom.

Just not the right kind for my family.

Rebel's gone quiet, and it's not until we've stepped outside that I understand why. Ruin is holding him hostage, pressing his chest and face flat against the brick side wall as he fights to break free. Thanatos is nowhere to be found, even now, and it takes me a second to understand why.

"Do you want me to shoot?" he asks, still hidden from view. A perfect hit man.

I lean down to whisper in Celia's ear. "It's your call, beautiful."

She clenches and unclenches her jaw, staring mutely into the busy traffic on the street in front of us. The streetlight changes from green to red, then back to green again before she speaks. "No," she says finally, closing her eyes. A silent tear tracks down her cheek before she hastily brushes it away. "I want her to remember the day she ruined her life for good." Pulling her cell phone from her pocket, she dials her brother's number and leaves a quick voicemail for him to call her when he gets the message and to avoid all contact with their mom.

Gently swinging her around until we're facing one another, I cup her warm cheek in my palm. "Are you sure about this?" Cutting off our dad was easy for us—but we had each other as a support system, and our father never was one to begin with.

Celia's been relying on her mother for years. It's not an easy tie to break.

Nodding, she swallows hard. "I think I've always known that she wasn't good for me. This was the proof I've been too afraid to see."

Rebel crashes into Celia from the side, wrapping her tightly in his arms and murmuring words of encouragement in her ear. "You're so fucking strong, baby, so strong. We can still go in there and fuck her shit up. Just say the word. I promise, I'll make it hurt."

Although I'm annoyed that he stole her from me, I'm grateful when she laughs. "I don't want you to do that, Rebel." She meets Ruin's gaze from over Rebel's shoulder. "You either, okay?"

He's taken to wearing his mask in public, and a part of me withers to see it. I wish he'd not give a damn about his appearance, but I know there are likely more layers to his rationale than I realize. Grunting, he acknowledges her request.

Thanatos finally arrives, jogging across the parking lot toward us. "She's still sitting at the table. I think she's in shock."

"Let her rot," Rebel huffs angrily. "*Now,* can we go home?" He slips his hands into Celia's dress pockets and caresses her hips, earning a blushing smile from our woman. All four of us stare at her, waiting for her call on where to go next. After the bullshit she just experienced on her mother's behalf, we're all on the same page about the rest of the day.

Let Celia decide how she wants to decompress, if at all.

Shaking her head, she releases a long exhale. "We're not done yet, are we? We still have step two to complete."

"We're still on step one," I clarify, licking my lips. Thanatos meets my gaze over Celia's head and nods. We talked about this at length outside of Ruin's door this morning so that he would hear the plan, too. After flaunting Celia around the city, we need to ensure that our father takes the bait and comes for her. If not tonight, then tomorrow night, or the next, or the *next*. No matter how long it takes, we'll catch the bastard, and we'll make him suffer.

"Pretending that everything is normal?"

Rebel murmurs the *real* reason we're parading Celia around the city in between a series of kisses across her jawline. "Putting you on display, baby. You're our arm candy until our dad comes out of hiding."

Her jaw pops open. "You can't be serious."

Thanatos crosses his arms over his chest as he comes to a stop behind her. "I don't joke. This is the plan, Princess. You agreed to do whatever it takes."

"It won't take long," I assure her, turning her face back toward me. "He's getting impatient. Making mistakes. It'll be easy to grab him once he's stepped out of the shadows."

I glance at Ruin, gauging his response. We all agreed that when the time came, we would let Ruin make the killing blow. It's only right, after everything our dad has put him through. My youngest brother stands completely still, looking out of place against a cafe backdrop, but without an ounce of discomfort, even in broad daylight. His eyes are trained on Celia, like she's the only thing keeping him anchored to the present. I doubt he's truly listening to our conversation, lost in the fog of his thoughts about Celia.

He's been doing that a lot—losing pieces of himself.

I only hope that no matter what happens, she can help him find whatever it is he's been looking for—whether that means regaining what he's lost, or creating something new to fill the void.

CHAPTER 10

RUIN

MY BROTHERS ENJOY WATCHING Celia in the daylight. Rebel and Rage take turns escorting her around the city, going nowhere in particular to leave her scent all over. A picture taken here, an ice cream cone purchased there. It's almost like they're tourists basking in each other's attention rather than the attention of the city.

For me, Celia always glows brightest in the dead of night.

After taking a heavy hit from my joint, I exhale the smoke from my lungs as slowly as possible, letting the burn settle my nerves. Funny thing, the feeling of burning alive. I sense flickers of it every time I take a pull, like a nightmare on the verge of collapsing around this fragile reality we call life. I can picture it—the walls collapsing, the rubble and smoke billowing into the air, the intensity of heat rolling across my skin and the bright, blinding light of it all singing my eyes.

Walking through the city almost felt like burning,

too, with my eyes stinging from the sunlight. Hours later, in the relative calm of the club's waking hours, my skin still pricks with the memory of it.

I drown out all feeling left in my body with the weed.

Rage is talking to Celia at his golden throne, a black leather monstrosity that he insists adds class to the club's atmosphere, when all it does is make him look like a kinky asshole. Behind them sits the shining golden cage he had installed after Celia ran away—quarter-thick bars tower ten feet high, where they're cut off by a paneled ceiling. You could easily install hooks to hang ropes or a swing inside, but Rage was never one for theatrics. The only item inside that cage is a silken pillow for Celia to kneel on.

Not that she ever will.

Even from a distance, I can see the anger burning in her eyes as they argue about the cage. Their voices raise high enough that club members are giving them a wide berth—even Fox, the red-headed VIP whose cherry red Ferrari Rebel took for a joy ride, keeps her distance. Tonight, she has two of her toys on leashes, parading both men around like pets.

I imagine that's how Rage wants Celia to behave. Like his pet. The heart-shaped pendant lying across Celia's throat gleams in the light as she turns her head away from Rage to scan the crowd.

I wonder if she's looking for me.

Thanatos walks over to me, slipping out of the shadows much like how I usually do. He's covered head-to-toe in the riot gear he picked up from the Dolohov job, minus the helmet. I take in his appearance, but so do a handful of thirsty passerby, a few of them bold enough to consider approaching before they realize that I'm standing next to him. Once they see me, they scamper away like vermin.

"You shouldn't be smoking," Than tells me, frowning as I bring the joint to my lips. "It'll slow your reaction time."

I ignore him, focusing instead on Celia. She's slipped down the stairs from Rage's throned stage to approach Fox, the two girls now engaged in conversation. They hug, like they're suddenly best friends, and travel to the bar together.

Hmm. Celia is playing her part as bait well. The rhinestones on her sheer top sparkle like diamonds, the black bralette covering her breasts hardly modest, more like a bikini. Her tits spill over the top, like it's a few sizes too small, and I picture the tight band digging into her soft skin. When she undresses in a few hours, she'll have red bands covering her ribs like halos, and my brothers will no doubt want to smooth them out with their fingertips. They always find ways to touch her.

But she always finds ways to touch *me*.

I'm not sure that I enjoyed her touch at first. It was foreign and warm, sending flickers of heat and tension rippling through my muscles. But the sensations were new, sparking a curiosity not only in how I was feeling— but how she reacted to my touch.

"*Krosotka* has always been responsive," I murmur,

putting out the joint on my thigh and slipping it into my pocket.

Thanatos follows my gaze across the room, his expression hardening once he realizes who has my focus. "We're not here to fuck, Ruin."

I nod toward all the guests in the room thinking the opposite. "They are."

"We're not them."

Although I've never been close to Thanatos, there has always been a part of me that understands him. Both of us are exceptional killers, one out of necessity and one out of fondness. Even now, this situation with Celia feels like it's born from those same tendencies—my brothers and I are with her because we like her, whereas Thanatos is only here because we've required it of him.

"What will you do when this is over?" I flick my gaze to his, noting the way his eyes have clouded. He stares at Celia, his body as tense as a tripwire waiting to be triggered. He doesn't want to be here, that much is clear. "We won't keep you." I push my gloved hands into my pockets and lean back against the cold wall. "If you want to go, you can go."

His jaw tightens. "It's not that simple."

Nodding, I hum to myself. It never is.

Things in our family have always been complicated and messy. I'm sure that in another life, Thanatos would be as far away from here as possible, leaving the city—hell, the country—to find some other purpose that doesn't involve taking orders from powerful men. Then again, he and Ezra were always a dynamic duo, even before I was old enough to recognize it.

"How are things with you and Ezra?" I ask, curious.

Than blinks, turning away from Celia to face me. "Why?"

I hum again. Why *am* I asking?

"He seems like a brother to you," I finally surmise, tilting my head. They're closer in age than I am to Thanatos, and surely Ezra doesn't have as fucked up of a past as I do. I doubt he has as much baggage suffocating him in his sleep.

I bet Ezra Reinoff sleeps like the dead.

Then again, the few times my boss and I have spoken about my targets, he's been a man of few words. Not guarded, exactly, but quiet. If Rage weren't so volatile, I imagine that he and Ezra would be alike in their sense of duty to the bratva and its *pakhan*. As it stands, Ezra and Thanatos likely have the most in common out of the four of us.

Hence why Ezra is more suited to be Thanatos's brother than me. The fact that Than and I share a bloodline doesn't mean shit when our bloodline is laced with poison.

My gaze wanders over to Celia again, up her long legs to those tiny, pleather shorts she's wearing. It's warm in the club by design, making it easier for people to shed their inhibitions as they strip naked in front of strangers. Tonight, however, none of our regulars are wearing masks, and that includes Celia.

I like it when she doesn't hide from me.

New guests to *Midnight* seem to think that my mask is a costume, a few of them smiling at me like they think I want to fuck them, or that they want to fuck me. But I've never been one to indulge in the flesh—and I'm not about to start tonight.

Flashbacks of that morning in Celia's bed hover in the back of my mind, a ripple of heat pooling deep in my gut. It's been happening more often lately, like the time spent hovering over Celia's naked body has unlocked something within me. I don't dare think—I don't dare *hope*—that it's a piece of me that has been lying dormant all these years, waiting to be brought back to life.

A piece of me lost, now found.

I drag in a quick lungful of air and squeeze my aching eyes shut. All of this is too much. My body is still recovering, taking its time to heal, or maybe it never was healed to begin with, and now we're merely feeling out what scraps are left to salvage. There can't be much left worth keeping.

"Are you okay?" Than asks, hovering closer. He's blocking off the rest of the room with his body, using every square inch of muscle and bone and armor to shield me from prying eyes. He may not realize that he's doing it, but I've seen both of my brothers' own protective tendencies enough times to recognize it here with Thanatos.

My brothers' best defense is their offense, both of them striking out before any of us can get injured. But Thanatos, my half-brother, must take more after his mother than our father, because his defense *is* a literal shield.

I'm starting to think that we might need that in our lives.

Tentatively, I reach out and touch his arm, allowing myself to feel his strength and to siphon some of it into my body. The doctors have always told me that the key to a long, healthy life is all about vitamin intake and exercise, but I've killed plenty of people to know that having a perfect body isn't what gives you a long life.

It's having a sound mind.

Mine is anything but *sound*.

I shake my head to drown out the static, sighing once my heartbeat drums in my ears. It's a quick energetic exchange between the two of us, but it's enough for me to refocus on our mission. As much as I'd rather spend the entire night watching *Krosotka*, I'm supposed to be watching for our father instead.

We all are. Even as Rage summons Celia to sit in his lap on the throne, and even as she turns her nose up and walks the other way, bucking the plan, that's what we're supposed to be doing.

Keeping watch for the enemy, not for each other.

But I have a feeling that all five of us will struggle to reign in our desires when desire is the very thing *Midnight* thrives on, the very thread of it twisting through the air and ensnaring its victims like a siren's song.

"This isn't a good idea." I track Celia's path with my eyes, longing to follow her and knowing that it's inevitable, because *I will*. And so will my brothers. We're all doomed when it comes to our woman. "We're all distracted."

Thanatos swallows hard, his gaze mirroring mine. "Yeah."

I pick at the edge of my face mask, itching to take it off. Ever since the last fire, it's been harder and harder to keep it on. I feel like I'm suffocating within it—like it's no longer a prop, but it's fusing to my skin. "Rage will want to lock her in the cage if it means completing our mission." I drag my hand down Than's chest, feeling the thick bulge of his armor. It would be hard to pierce with a knife, maybe impossible, and bullets likely won't get through either. "You should go by Riot," I tell him, rapping my knuckles against an armored plate over his stomach.

He chuffs, taking a step back and avoiding my gaze. "What, so I can join the family legacy?"

"Yes."

The scar cutting through his upper lip pulls as he twists his mouth. He takes a breath like he's going to say something, then stops himself. "Yeah. Maybe."

I grunt, pulling away from him. In the bratva, names are important. Blood is important, too, both in the ties it creates between family lines and the blood one spills on the floor. Names and blood are what keep us together, and since Thanatos can't get any closer by blood, the only thing left is by name.

Riot can be ours.

Mine. My brothers'. Hers.

"You should let Thanatos die," I conclude, taking another step away from him to follow Celia. "Shouldn't you?"

I leave my half-brother to his thoughts, knowing that the decision should be as simple for him as it was for me, Rebel, and Rage.

Should be.

But I have a feeling that with Thanatos, there are a lot of things he *should* do that he holds himself back from.

CHAPTER 11

CELIA

WANDERING the city aimlessly all day hasn't left me in the mood to party tonight, yet the boys insist on attending the latest VIP event for *Midnight*. Further still, none of them aside from Ruin are wearing masks.

Myself included.

A blush is permanently tattooed across my face as I walk through the club, my heels clicking with every step I take. Thankfully, almost every woman here tonight is in heels, so hardly anyone looks my way as I pass by. It's when they notice my lack of a mask that they understand who I'm here with—the only other maskless people in the room—and suddenly, all their smiles are kept polite and their distance substantial.

The one exception is Fox, her kitsune mask and fiery hair making her easy to spot in the crowd. We exchange friendly smiles before Rage steals me away from the dance floor.

"You could have asked if you wanted to dance," I

huff, frowning at his vice grip on my wrist. Rage isn't listening, too intent on dragging me away from the other guests. Pain shoots up my wrist, making me yelp. "Hey, you're hurting me!" One glance at the tension in his shoulders tells me that not only is he being bullish, but he's not having a good time. "What's wrong? Is your dad—"

"No," Rage interjects, loosening his grip as he leads me up the short flight of stairs to the most prominent stage in the room. It's a simple black platform with red velvet curtains draped on either side, impossible to miss beneath the warm spotlight. A throne fit for a dark king sits dead center, currently unoccupied. Just beside it, a gleaming gold cage similar to the one in the apartment upstairs sits empty, save for a single pillow resting in the center.

"I'm not going in there," I say immediately, returning his frown. I slip my wrist from his hand and lace our fingers together. "Tell me what's wrong."

Rage's eyes scan the crowd, his aura moody and dark. "He's not here," he says flatly. "He should be here. We're all here. Why isn't he here?" Looking at me, he pauses in thought, takes a deep breath, and pulls me into his chest. "You look stunning."

"You always say that."

"It's always true." He traces his thumb over my knuckles. "I don't know what's taking him so long."

"Well, was he a punctual man?"

"What?"

I purse my lips. "Your dad. Was he always on time, or was he always late?"

Rage chokes on a bitter laugh. "He'd never even show up." He slips his free hand beneath my shirt to palm my bare waist. "What are you getting at, *krosotka*?"

I shrug one shoulder and turn my face to survey the room in the same way he just did. "All I'm saying is, we keep expecting him to show up to a party he hasn't been invited to, when he's never shown up for anything before in his life. Why would he be here? Just because I'm here?" Shaking my head, I spot Ruin and Thanatos speaking to each other across the room. "There are too many of you and only one of him. If he knows that all four of you are with me, he won't jump in to grab me. It's too risky. Every woman he's taken, weren't they alone? On dates?" I swallow, thinking of Sara. She was alone at my boutique when she was taken. Maybe she was getting ready for a date with her boyfriend, even, when Rage's dad showed up and derailed her plans—possibly, her life. "It's not fair," I murmur, leaning into Rage's warmth. "All they wanted was a little company, or love, or a future, you know? And now it's been taken from them."

All because they had the misfortune of looking like me.

A shiver runs down my spine, and I press my forehead to Rage's chest. Breathing deep, I inhale his scent and try to let it soothe the ache in my heart.

"It's not your fault." Rage cradles the back of my head and runs his fingers through my long hair. "None of this is your fault."

"It feels like it's my fault."

"No." Gently tilting my head back, Rage stares into my eyes, the cut of his jawline sharp as a knife. He swallows, making his Adam's apple bob in the neon glow of the club. "It's my fault. I'm the one who demanded to have you, and the only reason my father is targeting any of these women is because I *do* have you. Because *we* do." Sighing, he closes his eyes. "But accepting blame doesn't solve anything. We need to kill the bastard before he gets to anyone else."

Sorrow surrounds my body like a cold morning fog spreading across the countryside, blanketing my limbs much the same way it might blanket a field of wheat. It's a heavy feeling that makes me want to be anywhere but here. Because as much as Rage might blame himself for his father's actions, I blame *myself* for everything having to do with Sara's disappearance.

Her murder, a nasty little voice in my head taunts. *You aren't going to save her, because there will be nothing left to save.*

Or what's left may not want to keep living.

"I need a drink," I mutter, giving Rage my best attempt at a smile. "Want anything?"

His eyes narrow as he scrutinizes my expression. "What's wrong, Celia?"

I swallow the truth as I pull free from his arms. "I need a drink," I repeat, hopping down the steps as quickly as I can.

A strong drink. A *very* strong drink.

My journey to the bar is quickly interrupted by a

familiar face. "Look at you! What a babe you've become." Fox smirks as she approaches me, leading two men behind her on leashes. I try not to stare and fail miserably, so I'm grateful when she envelops me in a hug. It means I won't have to puzzle through why the men with her are wearing only black collars, boxer-briefs, and matching wolf masks.

Then again, *I'm* wearing a collar, too.

The gold heart pendant feels heavy against my throat. "Your mask is gorgeous," I tell her, marveling at the red swirls painted across its white base. She's wearing a matching white silk kimono with a red sash tied around her waist. "Do you come to all of these events?"

"Every single one." She smiles beautifully and loops her arm through mine. "You were headed to the bar, weren't you?" Taking the first step, she leads me to the bar and perches on one of the padded stools, looping the leashes around her wrist. The men trailing behind her come to a stop at her side while she ignores their presence. She catches me staring and laughs.

Mortified, I'm quick to apologize. "I'm so sorry! I've just never, um, seen anything quite like it." My face heats, and I quickly down the first shot the bartender slides our way. We haven't ordered, but I don't care. "Keep them coming," I tell him, lifting my empty glass to signal him.

Fox smiles as she sips her alcohol. "So tell me, how are things in paradise? I hear that you live upstairs with all four of them now."

My heart stutters. How many people know that I'm

staying here, and with *four* men? "How did you hear that?"

She taps her bright red manicure against the edge of her glass. "I might not be Russian, but I know a thing or two about how this place works." Leaning over to whisper in my ear, she says, "I'm friends with Liara, their manager. She's the one who organizes these events." Sitting back on her stool, she tilts her head to the side. "You haven't met her?"

"I've been a bit—" How should I describe navigating three men's traumatic pasts? Instantly locking eyes with Thanatos from across the room, I inhale sharply as goosebumps trail down my arms, our prior collision inside the weapons room sending mixed signals to my body. Hot, cold, *feverish*. I swallow hard and quickly turn back to Fox.

She's wearing an amused smirk on her painted lips. *Shit.* Am I that easy to read?

"I've been, um, preoccupied." It's not only three men's trauma that I'm dealing with now, but four.

Apparently, that's amusing as hell to a woman like Fox. "I'll say." She lifts her glass and clinks it against mine. "To complications, then. May they be easy to bed and hard once they get there."

I laugh so hard that the vodka burns my nose.

"Speaking of complications, one of yours has come to visit." Fox winks at someone over my shoulder. "Hey there, handsome. Want a drink?"

Carefully spinning my chair around, I come face to face—well, mask—with Ruin. "Hey," I breathe, reaching for his hand. "What are you doing over here? Weren't you just with—" I glance behind him, then around the perimeter of the room. If Thanatos is nearby, he's out of my immediate vantage.

"I want you to dance." Ruin ignores Fox's greeting and takes a step closer to me, running his gloved hands up my thighs as he slips between them. "Will you dance for me, *krosotka*?"

My body warms from deep inside, spreading through my chest and deep beneath my belly. "Okay," I breathe, suddenly eager to please him. Although he's been going out into the city with us, I can tell it's a drain on his energy. His body is still healing, despite any wishful thinking he and his brothers might have. "But only if you dance with me."

Ruin is silent for a long moment. I don't know what I was thinking, telling him that. Of course he won't dance with me. I doubt he's ever danced in his life, and it's not like I'm an expert, either. "Forget I said anything—"

Slowly, he slides his hands over my hips and pulls me out of my chair, lowering me carefully to the ground. My heels click on the hardwood, but I can barely hear them over my thundering heart. "Okay," he says finally, dipping his head to whisper in my ear. "Take off your shoes."

I lean back and blink up at him. "What?"

"Your shoes." He taps my heels with the toes of his boots. "Take them off."

Following his instructions, I lift my feet one by one

and unstrap my heels, affixing them together and peering over my shoulder at Fox. "Could you—"

"Happy to," she purrs, taking the shoes from me before I can finish asking her to hold them for me. "Have fun, you two." Winking, she spins me back around, right into Ruin's arms. He catches me easily, looking as stiff as I've ever seen him as he peels me away from the bar.

"You don't have to," I say quickly, hating that I'm making him uncomfortable. "Seriously, I shouldn't have asked."

"It's what you want," he answers simply. "You should get what you want, *krosotka*."

So should you, I want to say. After a life of having things taken from him, he must be desperate to be willingly given something in return.

This is my chance to repay him for...

Well, everything.

As we step onto the dance floor, the other guests trickle away like falling water, clearing a path for us. The music is loud, thrumming with a heavy bass that vibrates through the floors. I watch as Ruin unlaces his boots and tosses both his socks and shoes to the side, joining me in barefoot bliss. The floors are cool on my feet, and I can only imagine what they feel like beneath his bandaged soles.

"Are you ready?" I ask, surprised when he suddenly removes his gloves, then even more surprised when he slowly unbuttons his shirt, revealing the fresh bandages across his shoulders and torso. Rebel and I have been working together to keep them clean, so they're not new for me.

But they are for everyone else.

Muffled whispers and gasps, a few laughs, and some cat-calling whistles fill the room. Ruin pays none of them any mind, stepping up to me with only his black cargo pants and leather belt strapped to his hips. The hunting knife that he used on me a few days ago is strapped tightly to his thigh, a reminder that even if he looks vulnerable with all the bandages and scars trailing across his body, he's anything but.

Meeting his eyes, I grab the bottom of my sheer top and pull it over my head, tossing it into the pile with his shirt and shoes. I leave my bralette on, but it leaves little to the imagination, especially with such an experienced audience.

Still.

If Ruin is willing to strip down for me, then I'm willing to do the same for him.

Slowly, I close the distance between us. I'm not much of a dancer, but I've taken enough lessons to know that if it's only the two of us out here, it doesn't have to be dancing in the traditional sense.

Professionals tell a story with their bodies. They move not only to the music, but to each other, feeling the ebb and flow between their bodies and learning each other's rhythms.

I place my open palm on his chest and push, sending him back a step so that I can fill the space. Then I curve around his body, trailing my fingers over his collarbone, then across his shoulder, down his arm and wrist, until my fingertips brush the soft center of his hand. Coming up behind him, I press a kiss to his shoulder, then to the back of his neck—to the scars peeking out over his bandages.

He inhales sharply and turns, catching my waist and dragging me against his body. Staring into my eyes, he takes another deep breath, his chest heaving.

"It's okay," I murmur, sliding my palms up the sides of his neck and over, until I can wrap my arms around him. "Just breathe. Breathe with me."

We move to our own beat, neither of us listening to the electric guitar riffs or pounding drums, focusing instead on each other. The touch of his hand on my hip or across my ribs, his fingers dragging against my flesh. I weave my hands into his hair and pull, earning a grunt that doesn't sound nearly as pained as it would for any other man. I scrape my nails over his scalp, and he groans deep in his chest, panting harshly against his mask.

Leaning up on my tiptoes, I rasp in his ear. "Do you want to stop?" My heart's beating on overdrive, my body extraordinarily sensitive to his touch, his breath, every inch of his skin touching mine. He's hot to the touch, his exposed skin flushed a peachy pink.

He *growls*, lifting me up off the floor to hold me over his hips, aligning our bodies so that I can feel every hard inch of him pressing against my core. "Does it feel like I want to stop, *krosotka*?"

Wanton desire pulses through my veins, pooling between my thighs and making it hard to speak without my voice shaking. "N-no," I pant, biting my bottom lip. "But are you sure—"

"Stop asking," he snarls. "I am as sure about this as I am about breathing. *Stop. Asking.*" Without warning, he wraps his arms tight around me and drops to his knees with a hard *bang*, catching me by such surprise that I *squeal.* My heart pounds as I wrap my thighs around his hips and hold on to him for dear life.

With a chuckle, he lowers my back to the cool hardwood floor and scrapes the edge of his hard face mask against my neck, sparking fire across my skin. When he pulls away, he stares at whatever mark he's made, his dark eyes glowing with desire. "Your skin," he mumbles, pulling at my calves so that he can loosen my grip enough to reach between us. Once he's made room, he slips his hand over his belt and undoes the buckle, pulling the leather free and snapping it in his hands.

My body jolts at the sound, my nipples pebbling into tight peaks. "What are you—"

"Shh," he beckons, settling his hips over mine and rocking, groaning at the friction it creates.

Pleasure shoots down my spine, making my eyes flutter. *Fuck.* That shouldn't feel so good. I trap my bottom lip between my teeth as Ruin laces my hands together in a prayer pose, then binds my wrists together with his belt. Cinching it tight, he tucks the end through one of the loops and tests its hold, nodding once he's satisfied.

"I want to feel you," he murmurs, planting his palms on the back of my thighs and *pushing*, forcing my knees closer to my chest. I gasp at the stretch, knowing that I'll pay for it in the morning, but unwilling to tell him to stop.

He latches onto the sound, his head tilting to the side. "Does that hurt?"

"A-a little."

Releasing one of my legs, he snaps open the front button on my shorts and tears them open one-handed. Before we came downstairs for the evening, the brothers all agreed that even if no one was going to see what I was wearing underneath my clothes, it needed to be sexy so that I would feel sexy, a concept that they were clearly proud of. I didn't have the heart to tell them that women were the ones who came up with that idea long before they had, but from the way Ruin's pupils dilate upon seeing the scarlet lace hidden beneath my shorts, I have a feeling that the boys may have been lying about that part.

They really wanted me to wear lace for themselves.

Ruin grabs the hunting knife strapped to his thigh and pulls it from its sheath. "Stay still," he tells me, pressing the flat side of the knife against my thigh. It's cold, causing goosebumps to form around its touch. Staring at my raised flesh, Ruin tips the knife onto the dull edge and carves upward, applying enough pressure for me to feel the blade without the danger of it cutting my skin. He hums while he works, carving some kind of design into my flesh, the knife criss-crossing across my thigh, then over my stomach, around my bellybutton, then back down over the swell of my belly. He tips the sharp point to my panties, slipping it beneath the band and snapping the elastic with a flick of his wrist. With a grunt, he tears through the flimsy fabric, then switches focus to the black pleather digging into my thighs.

Booty shorts might be sexy for the first hour or two, but they sure as shit aren't comfortable after that.

"Cut them off," I whine, lifting my hips. My pussy throbs as he obliges, grabbing hold of one half of the zipper, pulling the material tight, and sawing through the middle. He tears through the rest, hastily shoving the fabric over my thighs so that it falls to the floor beneath us. His blade nicks my skin at the very end, a sudden prick of sharp pain that quickly turns into a burning heat.

Ruin freezes, his body going completely still.

"I'm okay," I promise, wriggling on my back so that he knows how serious I am about that. Yes, the knife is scary, or it's supposed to be—*fuck*, I don't know, I just want my clothes off! "Please don't stop—"

His eyes snap to mine and he hisses through his teeth, suddenly grinding his erection against my pussy. I drag in a thick lungful of air as he digs in his heels and ruts against me, neither of us actually naked, but both of us on the same page about what we want.

"Take them *off*," I whine for a second time. "*Please*, take them off. Touch me, Ruin, I'm so—I'm so hot, baby. Please."

With a groan, he drops the knife and lowers his body over mine. Wedging his hand between my thighs, he buries his fingers inside what's left of my panties and cups my sex, sliding his fingers through my slick folds. "Always so wet," he pants, thrusting his hips. The pressure pushes his fingertips past the threshold and inside of me, making my eyes roll back as he finally starts moving, working my pussy with his fingers and thrusting wildly, lost to a rhythm I can no longer hear. His cock grinds against my body, slotting in the curve where my thigh meets my pelvis, while I attempt to fuck myself on his fingers. It's a fight for friction and pressure, both of us demanding more without working together to achieve it.

"*Fuck*," he moans, his body trembling as he smothers mine. I feel his cock pulse with his release, the sticky seed caught in his boxers. I'm close but not *that* close, and my need tumbles past my lips as incoherent phrases and moans that come just short of begging.

Once the blood rushing in his ears settles, Ruin realizes that I'm still writhing beneath him and surges back to life, burying his fingers to the knuckle and stretching my pussy, going deeper than he's ever dared before. "You will come for *me*," he growls, panting hotly against his mask. Grinding the heel of his palm against my clit, he makes me scream as pleasure dips into pain, the pressure too much, too hard—his fingernails too sharp, carving me up inside. But through it all, the pleasure barrels through my body like a freight train, an invisible force that can't be stopped.

I suck in lungfuls of air as my pleasure crests, tears stinging my eyes as Ruin wrenches an orgasm from deep within me. My body convulses as my pussy clenches hard, a silent scream catching in my throat as I come.

Rather than praise me for how well I came for him, Ruin hums in the back of his throat and drags his fingers through my soaked folds, enjoying the feel of my body submitting to his. I breathe as deeply as I can, willing the stars from my eyes as I come back into my body and mind.

Laughter floats through the air, as do wet, sucking sounds and the slap of skin on skin, and I turn my face to the side to find that not only are Ruin and I writhing on the floor together, but so are a half dozen other couples, some of them watching the carnal pleasures evolving around them while others are so focused on chasing their own pleasure that the world is as lost to them as it was to me and Ruin.

I blow air against the sweat on Ruin's neck, grateful when he shivers, waking from his own lustful haze. Slowly, he pulls his fingers from my pussy and drags them against my stomach, smearing my skin with my desire. "Soon," he rumbles, palming the band of fabric over my chest while he buries his face in the crook of my neck. His mask cuts into my skin, one of the buckles digging into the soft flesh above my collarbone. "Soon, *krosotka*, you will be *mine.*" His fingers dig between my breasts, pressing hard against my sternum.

Closing my eyes, I try not to let him feel the anxious stutter of my heart, the way it skips two beats and ramps up fast.

If *this* isn't what makes me his, then what is?

He exhales slowly and chuckles, finally lifting himself onto his knees to untie his belt from around my wrists. "You will like that, won't you?" Blood rushes to my hands, making me gasp. He squeezes my fingers. "It was *me* you cried for as you drove these fingers into your cunt every night for weeks, wasn't it?"

It takes me a moment to realize that he's talking about the *before*—all the long nights in between when he first appeared in my kitchen with my invitation to *Midnight* and the actual event when he and his brothers officially claimed me. It feels like a lifetime ago—like I was someone else, chasing a high I never realized how much I needed.

That's how these men feel to me—like a new life.

Chuckling, Ruin pulls my fingertips to his abdomen, letting me feel the heat of his scarred flesh. "Am I everything you hoped for? The man of your dreams?"

I can't read his mind to find out what he wants me to say, so all I can be is honest.

"I don't know," I breathe, staring beyond the faceless mask to the man hiding underneath. "But I want to find out."

His eyes flash silver. "Then we will."

I echo his words, feeling the weight of them in not just my heart, but my soul. "Then we will."

CHAPTER 12

REBEL

"HE DID *WHAT*?"

"Don't be so surprised," Rage grumbles, sipping his disgusting black coffee. "He's been watching how you interact with her. It was only a matter of time before he did something on his own."

"I'm not surprised." Grinning, I pop a strip of greasy bacon into my mouth and chew the salty goodness. "I knew he had it in him. I'm just—*wow*. I can't believe I missed it!" A pang of regret almost takes my joy away —*almost*. But nothing will top my little brother damn near getting some! And in *public*, too!

"He's earning his stripes." I slam my hand down on the countertop, my body brimming with excitement. "Man, I can't believe I missed it." I was right next door in the other ballroom. Someone could have easily come to get me before the show was over. It's not like losing one hand of poker would have decimated the whole night's earnings.

"You were busy," Thanatos says nonchalantly, like I don't already know. "It was an important mission."

"*Mission*," I sneer, crinkling my nose. "Like babysitting a bunch of old fucks actually counts as a mission."

"It does when it funds the next phase of the plan." Snapping his newspaper shut, Than scowls over the kitchen island at me. "We can only pull so many funds from the bratva's coffers before Mikhail closes the bank. We need your winnings for Celia's dress. She has to be a showstopper next week."

Rage spears a slice of banana with his fork. "She already *is* a showstopper."

I nod in agreement. "If your head wasn't so far up your ass, you'd know."

Thanatos's scowl deepens. "What I think about her doesn't matter. It's what *he* thinks."

Rolling my eyes, I scoff. "Dad doesn't need to think that she's a smokeshow. He's going to try to kill her regardless of what she's wearing. The new dress was your idea. *I* still think she should wear one of her own designs." Celia has been working herself stupid over these gowns she creates, wanting to make sure that all five or six of her clients look flawless at the upcoming charity gala. It's ridiculous that her invitation was revoked first thing this morning.

I bet her monster of a mother has something to do with it.

Scowling at my full cup of coffee, I slam my mug down, sloshing some over the rim. I voted to kill the bitch on sight the next time we run across her—likely at the very same gala she shut her own daughter out of—but everyone else veto'd that idea.

Except for Ruin. He never voted.

Tilting my head back, I stare at the ceiling toward his bedroom. If I can get Ruin alone with me, the two of us might be able to sneak off and gut Adella fucking Monrovia for being such a cunt. *Especially* if she's at the gala. Picture this: an old, crusty bitch is found stabbed to death and rolled up in one of those dusty velvet curtains, like in the movies. Or maybe we can find a trash chute and shove her bony ass down into the dumpster.

Celia would be none the wiser. It would be *fine.*

Snapping his fingers, Rage tries to catch my attention. "Hey. We are *not* killing anyone at the gala. Get that fucking look off your face."

I cross my arms. "Since when is killing someone at the gala off the table? That was never a rule."

"Since we became guests. I got all five of us tickets so that we can escort Celia without having to sneak in."

Thanatos doesn't seem pleased with the news. "Under what names?"

Rage stabs another piece of fruit, some kind of orange square, before setting his fork down. "I couldn't exactly tell them to put Rage, Rebel, and Ruin on the guest list, could I?"

My annoyance ticks up five fucking notches. "Uh, yeah, you could have. With the amount of money I grabbed last night, you could have told them you were Queen fucking Latifah, and they still would have let you in. I am *not* going under another name."

Rage grits his teeth. "Don't be stupid. You *know* that bratva influence can only go so far. Showing up as Rebel won't win you any favors with this crowd. It'll make everything ten times more difficult. Remember when you stole that car from the police chief last year? That warrant is still out for your arrest, with your shit-eating grin all over the fucking pictures."

Ah, my first time in a Lamborghini.

"He's just mad that I fucked his wife better than him."

Thanatos stares at me without blinking. "You slept with the police chief's wife?"

"They were separated."

"Twice," Rage growls. "He slept with her *twice.*"

"I got you the security code for his computer, didn't I? What's the big deal, all of a sudden?" I glare at Rage, not sure where this is coming from or what it has to do with the gala next week.

Than and I both wait for Rage's reply. He chugs the rest of his coffee and pours a second cup. "We can't fuck this up. All of us have to blend in, or shit could go sideways in a second. We can't let Celia go in there alone. We *can't.* Ruin will be allowed in with his ticket, but you know he won't be comfortable in a crowd, especially if he can't wear his mask."

Clearing his throat, Than mutters under his breath. "He seemed pretty comfortable last night."

Fuck, I'm going to have to check the cameras to see what I missed. "They had a crowd?"

"The entire room," Than confirms, nodding. "Half

of them couldn't wait to tear their clothes off." He scratches the side of his neck and quickly looks away, grabbing his coffee mug and filling it to the brim.

Yeah, half the room, right. Himself included.

Snickering, I let it go. Teasing him won't get Rage off my back about this gala bullshit. "So we go in, schmooze all the rich city fucks, and make sure that Celia sparkles like a fucking diamond. What's the big deal? It's not like anyone will care about which man's attached to her hip when she's going to steal the spotlight."

Rage levels me with a look. "I don't want you to get arrested for being careless."

"Just bail me out like usual."

"He doesn't want you to be *alone*," Thanatos clarifies, nodding like he agrees. "We're vulnerable when we're alone."

My stomach churns at where this conversation is headed. "He wouldn't kill me," I mutter, frowning. "He has no reason to care about me at all." Although our father won the annual Shittiest Dad of the Year award ever since Than was born, he gave more shit to my brothers than to me. I guess being the middle child kept me under the radar.

"*We* care." Rage claps me on the shoulder. "He could come after any one of us if it makes splitting us up and getting to Celia easier."

Ugh. Why does revenge have to be so fucking complicated? You kill the guy, then it's over. *Boom.* Vengeance complete.

"Well, I still think that Celia should wear one of her own dresses. And the name thing? Fucking stupid."

I haven't thought of myself as anyone other than Rebel in a goddamn decade, and I'm not about to start now, no matter what Rage thinks.

When my fake ID finally arrives, I quickly decide that it's stupid.

Stupid, stupid, *stupid.*

The picture is clearly photoshopped. All of my tattoos have been scrubbed clean in the image, even the knife on the side of my neck. On the night of the gala, Celia helps me cover up the real ones with concealer, spending two fucking hours making all three of my brothers and me presentable. We go through at least three bottles of makeup, despite it being made for tattoo cover-ups. She says something about *blending* to make everything look even, whatever the fuck that means.

While she gets ready in Rage's bedroom, I stare at my reflection in my bathroom mirror, not liking what I see staring back at me. My lip piercing is lying on the counter instead of on my face where it belongs, and Rage forced me to get a haircut so that when I slick back my hair, it will actually stay in place without falling into my eyes. The barber shaved off the sides to give me some kind of a vintage gentleman look, but little did he know, I have a tattoo on my skull, too. It peeks out through what little remains on my sides, like a big old *fuck you* to my older brother.

I hope Rage notices and gets *really* fucking pissed about it.

Turning my head, I try to catch a glimpse of my ink. I got it shortly after officially joining the bratva, so it's no wonder Rage doesn't remember. He was too busy kissing Ezra's ass to pay attention to what I was doing half the time. The tattoo has faded over the years, but the joker card's fleshless skull is still grinning back at me, the bloodied knife he flicks over his head as red as the day it was inked.

If there's one thing I'm good at, it's playing people. They're too trusting of a pretty face, especially if that face knows how to win a lot of cash and have a good time.

Everyone at this pretend casino night event is about to have their bank accounts fucked hard, by yours truly.

I fiddle with the tie around my neck, the knot way too fucking tight on account of Rage's anal standards about our appearance for the evening. It pinches my neck like it wants to get me off at half price. Rolling my eyes, I loosen it so that I can actually breathe, then unroll my sleeve cuffs so that they hang over my wrists.

"Perfection is necessary," my ass.

The minute I've walked through those doors, I'm untucking my shirt and throwing the tie in the nearest trash can, appearances be damned. I've always been told that I have a roguish charm, and people will be able to see through me if I look all dolled up like some pompous billionaire.

I won't pretend to be something—or someone—I'm not.

Which brings us back to the name dilemma.

I place my palms on the bathroom counter and lean over the sink, dangling my head and closing my eyes. Taking a deep breath, I will myself into thinking that the name doesn't matter. It's just a word. So what if people think I'm *Emil* tonight? It won't change who I really am.

I'm still *me*. I'm still Rebel.

My birth name doesn't fucking change that.

There's a knock on my bathroom door before it swings open, and the most beautiful fucking woman steps into view. She's not fully dressed yet, wearing a matching set of black lace panties, bra, and a little band around her thigh that conceals one of the tiniest knives I've ever seen. Fiddling with a piece of jewelry in her hands, Celia doesn't look up as she approaches me. "Rebel, can you help me clasp this?"

My heart soars at being her go-to choice. "Yes," I reply eagerly, dropping everything I'm doing to walk over to her. I hold out my open palm until she drops the diamond necklace in my hand. When she finally looks up, her eyes widen.

"You like it?" I ask, smirking as her eyes rake across my new look. I might not feel like me without my tattoos and piercings, but I sure as hell look as hot as I usually do.

Her eyes narrow for a second before she reaches up and ruffles my hair, undoing the gentleman look with a simple brush of her fingers. Carefully styling a few strands to fall over my forehead while the others tumble back, she smiles. "There. Now you're as gorgeous as me."

"Cheeky!" Folding over her body, I bury my face in the crook of her neck and inhale her perfume. All it takes is a slow skim of my lips over her skin for my cock to swell, and I'm dragging her body into mine. Nipping her delicate skin, I love the little gasp that falls from her lips.

"We don't have time," she sighs, hooking her fingers into my waistband. "C'mon, help me get ready. Rage is already throwing a fit over Ruin."

I steal a lingering kiss, slipping my tongue between her lips with a groan. "Let him stew, baby. I've always got time for you." I drop her necklace into my pocket and lift her, swinging her around until she's braced on the bathroom counter.

God, she's gorgeous. Her tits don't spill out of her bra like they normally do, but *fuck*, I so don't care. Running my tongue between them, I taste her skin, eager for more. "If I make you come," I murmur, flicking my gaze up to her face, "then you don't get to wear *these*—" I tug off her panties and slip them into my back pocket— "tonight." Spreading her thighs, I inhale her scent and choke on a moan. *Fuck*, she's delicious, and I haven't even tasted her yet.

Scooting her ass to the edge of the counter and dropping a folded towel to the tile floor, I drop to my knees and *finally* dive between her thighs, licking a stripe along her pussy and groaning. Her nails dig into my scalp as I spread her lips and go deeper, spearing her with my tongue before laving her clit with long, hard strokes. Celia keens, her back arching as she digs her heels into my shoulders, pulling me closer.

Fuck, she's into this. *I'm* into this. Why the hell have I been letting Rage do all the tongue work? Because he *claimed* it?

Her pussy gets wetter, drenching my mouth and chin, and I groan as my cock fills to bursting. I run the pads of my fingers along her entrance, teasing her, before getting to my feet and tearing at my belt. "Let me fuck you," I pant. "I want you dripping down your thighs all night, baby."

A *bang* behind me makes Celia jump, but I'm used to my brother's outbursts. "*Rebel*," Rage hisses, having burst into the room, "don't you dare!"

Freeing my cock, I rush to get inside our girl before he spoils our fun. Slotting myself against her heat, I grin at Rage's reflection as I push inside. "Ohhh," I groan, grabbing her hip to steady her. She's soaking wet and trembling, her legs quickly wrapping around my waist as I punch deeper, slotting myself fully inside of her. "Fuck, that's good. *Fuck*, baby, that's good."

I barely get another thrust in before Rage is snarling behind me like a rabid animal, clearly having some kind of tantrum.

I'm too far gone to care, balls deep and panting in Celia's ear. She slides her fingers through my hair, tugging on the strands until she's able to latch onto my mouth. I groan as she bites my bottom lip and sucks, taking over my mouth the same way I'm taking her pussy, hard and fast and *wet,* so goddamn wet. My balls draw up and I come fast, the softest whimper escaping past my lips as my cock jerks, filling her up just like I'd promised, each pump painting her walls with my cream.

She hums against my mouth, then grabs my chin and wrenches my face to the side. "You don't think you're done, do you?" She pants, locking her legs tighter around my hips. With both of her hands anchored to my shoulders, she grinds her pussy onto my cock, crying out as she hits the perfect spot. "*Yes,*" she moans, her nails digging into my back. "Yes, Rebel, right there. *God*, I need you to make me come. I need it so bad. Don't you want to make me come? You *promised*."

I drive into her again, gasping as a surge of pleasure rushes down my spine. "I will, baby, I promise." Shit. How long can I go? It doesn't matter—I *have* to keep going. She latches onto my neck and sucks, sending another spark of need straight to my balls. "S-stop," I whine, dropping my forehead onto her shoulder. "I can't —*fuck*."

Celia brings her lips to my ear, her voice as sinfully sweet as her cunt. "You'll come again for me, won't you?" She grinds her hips, gasping as she moves. "*Please* come for me. I need—I need *more*. Be a good boy and fill up my pussy."

Oh. My. God.

Within seconds, my body's convulsing for a second

time as she milks my cock. This time, she murmurs a repeated *yesyesyes* as she chases her own high, finally coming with a high-pitched cry that sparks across my skin like firecrackers. I drag in lungfuls of air, tasting her desire on my lips, my tongue, the heavy scent of sex filling the room.

"Well then," Rage rumbles somewhere in the distance, "you two get along *well*."

I can't help but laugh at my brother's burning jealousy. It's eating him alive.

"What's so fucking funny?"

Kissing a bright-eyed Celia before daring to meet my brother's glare in the mirror, I grin wolfishly at him. "Give it a rest, man. She's *ours*. If you want her, come get her." I press another kiss to Celia's lips, then to her flushed cheek. "Do you want him to fill you up, too, baby?"

I'm sure that Rage is tired of feeling like sloppy seconds, but it's not *my* fault that he's got a stick up his ass. If he'd let loose a little, I'm sure she'd open up to him as beautifully as she opens up for me. Hell, she's opening up to *Ruin*. If anyone can love that fucker, then there's hope for Rage, yet.

Rage cuts into the conversation before Celia can reply. "There's no time. Get dressed—both of you. And keep your clothes on." He smacks his palm against the door frame before leaving, no doubt needing to find a release of his own.

Celia traces her fingertips along my new fade, then runs her hands through my sweat-slicked hair. "Do you think he's mad at me?" she asks, her eyebrows pinching with worry. "I just—it's just that—" Sighing, she buries her face against my neck. "Things feel so easy with you, you know?"

I feel the exact same way.

"I know."

Slowly pulling away from her, I slide my cock out from her slick heat and admire the mess we've made. I almost feel bad about taking her panties—but I *really* want her to be thinking of me all night long, no matter whose arm she's on. Slipping my fingers between her thighs, I carefully gather the cum leaking from her slit and push it back inside, hoping that it takes.

I know that Rage insists on being the first of us to knock her up, but sometimes I think...

Maybe I want it to be me.

After helping Celia off of the counter and finally latching her necklace in place, I let her in on a secret. It's actually why Rage came to find her in the first place, but I was too distracted to remember until post-nut clarity hit. *Oops.*

"He has a surprise for you," I admit sheepishly, feeling a liiiiittle guilty for once. "That's why he came in here."

"Oh," she breathes, flushing with embarrassment. "I guess I should, uh, go find him."

Grabbing her hand as she tries to leave, I pull her back in for a slow kiss, hoping that she knows that even though Rage is struggling with his feelings, I don't regret anything. "Hey," I murmur, holding her tight in my arms. My heart pounds harder the longer I look into her eyes, and I suddenly forget what I was trying to say. "Um, I just wanted to say... that..."

I love you.

The words slam into my chest, and I'm not prepared for the overwhelming wave of emotion that follows.

Celia waits patiently for me to finish what I'm trying to say, and that makes it harder to remember anything other than those three little words.

"I don't regret anything," I blurt out, mentally cursing myself for dropping the bag. Would she even want to hear me say it? That I love her? Is now the right time? Does she even feel the same way about me?

"I don't regret anything, either." Kissing my cheek, she smiles. "I never regret anything with you, Rebel. You make me feel..." Her hazel eyes glitter like starlight. My heart kicks against my ribs like a bass drum.

Ba-dum.

"...alive. I really love spending time with you."

I swallow the lump in my throat and match her sweet smile with my own. "Yeah, me too." I kiss her again to keep myself from saying something even *more* stupid, like how she not only makes me feel alive, but how perfect I think she is for our family... and for *me*.

Rebel.

Emil.

Whoever I am when we're together.

That's what I love.

The person I become when she's around...

...and the person who makes it so easy to become him.

She slips out of the bathroom to go find Rage, and it's only then that I'm able to say the words that have been running through my head.

"I love you."

CHAPTER 13

CELIA

When I step out of Rebel's bedroom to look for Rage, I don't find him.

I find a dress.

Crimson petals cascade down a satin bodice, falling like autumn leaves onto the floor-length skirt, dyed in a gorgeous deep scarlet. Tiny jewels dangle from the petals like dewdrops, adding a sparkling overlay that makes me giddy with excitement as I play with the fabric in my hands, twisting it in the light to catch the dazzling indigo glimmers. Movement to my right catches my eye, and I quickly drop the dress to turn toward him. "Rage, did you—"

My eyes focus on a tall, muscular man that *almost* looks like Rage from a glance, but isn't.

"Thanatos," I breathe, brushing a strand of hair behind my ear. I clear my throat. "Have you seen Rage?"

It takes a second for him to respond, his gaze

hovering below my navel. "Left with Ruin," he rasps, mimicking me by clearing his throat. Averting his gaze, he runs a hand down his face and curses under his breath. "You should get dressed, Princess. You've got—" His ears turn red, the pop of color quickly trailing down his neck, then across his cheeks. "Ten minutes left." Like the others, he's dressed to the nines in a well-pressed suit, skipping the jacket for a dashing gunmetal gray vest and silver tie that matches the streaks in his hair. Although I helped apply makeup to cover his tattoos, I haven't seen him over the past hour or two while he got dressed, and the difference between the man I've sparred with on and off for days and the one standing before me is striking. But there are a few things that a suit can't cover up, the most prominent being the eternal sense of brooding that hovers around him like an aura, with the second being the short scar cutting through his upper lip.

He's drop-dead gorgeous, the little hints of danger amplifying my sudden attraction.

I suck in a breath and quickly look away, focusing on the dress again. "I was planning to wear a black evening gown to match everyone." That's why I chose black underwear. So that everything would match— "Ohmygod!"

My underwear.

Cum gushes out of my pussy as I clench every muscle in my body in a panic, hastily pulling the dress from the hanger to cover myself. Rebel still has my panties. I'm fucking naked in front of Thanatos.

"Why the *fuck* didn't you say anything!"

"It's your house!" he snaps, his eyes sparking as he glares at me from across the room. "So what if you're naked! Get fucking dressed, like I told you to!"

Groaning, flailing, *dying*, I clutch the dress to my chest and make a run for Rebel's bedroom, reaching for the door—

There is no door.

"For fucking sake!"

Rebel bursts from the bathroom, his hair as wild as his eyes. Half of his shirt is tucked in, and a cigarette dangles from his lips. A silver ring wraps around his bottom lip, an obvious show of defiance toward his older brother's orders for being clean-cut tonight. "What? What happened?" Spotting me, he looks between me and Thanatos through the doorway. "Did he finally bite?"

"What?" I jump back behind the wall, out of Thanatos's view. "No, I just—I went out there looking for Rage, and I—I'm naked! I didn't think he'd be here!"

Smirking mischievously, Rebel slinks toward me. "He's our driver, baby. Of course he's here. Did Rage and Ruin leave already?"

Thanatos barks out a harsh "yes!"

Rebel nods, not the least bit disturbed that his eldest brother just saw me half-naked and dripping with his cum. "You're starting the night with me, remember? Is that your dress?" He fondles the skirt before smacking my ass. "Damn, you're gonna look so good in that color."

Swatting his hand away, I shove him toward the open door. "Rebel! I need to get changed, or we'll be late!"

With a groan, he turns on his heel and wanders to the kitchen island where our shoes are laid out. The only ones left are my heels and Rebel's Oxfords. He brings them back to the bedroom and sits at the edge of the bed to put his on. After flicking ash from his cigarette, he points the tip at me. "A few minutes aren't gonna kill us. Relax, baby. We're gonna have a good time."

I get him to help me zip up, then I strap my heels and follow him into the living room. Thanatos is shaking car keys in his hand, his heel bouncing on the floor while he waits for us. "I've got your bag," he says flatly, shoving a clutch against my chest. "Lipstick, wet wipes, ibuprofen, tickets." He rattles off my list of requested items like it's a chore, moodily staring at my feet. "You forgot the shoes."

Huffing, I slam my heel down so that it clicks loudly. "I'm wearing them, Than."

He shakes his head. "No, *those.*" Grumbling, he pushes himself off the counter and crosses to the cage, grabbing a pair of heels I've never seen before from its base. "Size eight, diamond shimmer with a blue sparkle. They match your dress."

They're taller than the ones I was planning to wear, the wide-base heel a solid three inches high. Who picked all of these things for me? Was this Rage's surprise?

"Put them on so we can go."

There are no straps, so they're an easy fit. I lean on Rebel's shoulder as I slip them on. They actually fit like a glove, with a padded insole to make the night more bearable. Wearing brand new shoes to an event like this is going to be killer on my feet, no matter which pair I go with.

"Great," Thanatos deadpans, narrowing his eyes at me and Rebel before storming over to the front door. "We're finally ready. Let's go, lovebirds."

Grinning with excitement, Rebel takes my hand and leads us through the door, then down the hall to the grand staircase. Once we're at the top, he releases my hand and steps back to admire me from afar, whistling as he crouches for a better look at either my ass or my calves. "Damn, baby, you're a fucking bombshell in that dress."

I blush at the compliment, smoothing out the front of the gown. It's tight enough to show my curves, including the bump from my stomach. The bodice cuts a sweetheart neckline, with a selective strip of lace crawling up both sides of my chest and over my shoulders, trailing crimson petals down to my wrists. I was in such a rush to leave that I didn't check my reflection in the mirror, and now I regret it.

Shifting my skirt to peek at my heels through the high slit, I twist them in the light to admire the sparkle. Thanatos was right—there's a hint of blue every time I move, from both the dress *and* the shoes.

I glance back at Rebel from over my shoulder. "You coming?"

"In a minute," he murmurs, still staring at my ass. "I want to watch you walk away."

Rolling my eyes, I laugh as I carefully descend the stairs one at a time, keeping my skirts lifted and my chin held high. I don't have an audience, but feeling confident is key to our success tonight. I need to be as carefree as a young woman riding the highs of budding love should be, smiling and laughing and having the night of her life.

Once I'm halfway down the stairs, I realize that not only is Rebel watching me walk away, but Thanatos is staring up at me from the ground floor. Pinned between them, I feel my face flush with embarrassment. It's one thing to be confident in a room full of strangers—but catching the eye of not only your lover but his grumpy half-brother feels more intense.

Thanatos meets me at the last few stairs, gently taking my hand once we're at eye level. There's a bewilderment to his gaze, almost like he can't believe what he's seeing, much like how I can't believe what I'm feeling.

Butterflies.

My lips curve into a shy smile, the warmth of his hand sending tingles down my fingertips. "Care to give a girl a compliment?" Part of the plan for tonight is to spend time with each of them, Thanatos included, so that there are pockets of time when I'm alone in between transitions. I'm most nervous about being alone with him, honestly, especially after what happened in the armory.

We haven't talked about it, and I haven't told the others.

If I look close enough, I can almost see it in his eyes—that spark of wildfire desire that's close to catching, threatening to spread throughout his entire body. He swallows, takes a quick glance down my body, and exhales a broken chuckle. "You don't need a compliment from me, Princess." As I take another step, he murmurs, "you've already got one dripping down your legs."

I snap my eyes to his, catching the flash of burning need before he can hide it. We stare at each other for as long as we dare, neither of us moving. "Maybe I want one. From you."

He sucks in a breath, his gaze flicking to my lips. "I can't."

My heart pounds as I squeeze his fingers. "Why not?"

He leans closer, gently brushing his lips against my cheek in a whisper of a kiss. His warm breath tickles my nose as he rumbles his answer. "You're not mine."

In the next instant, everything except my beating heart and shaking knees is back to normal. Thanatos helps me down the last few steps, then releases my hand to make way for his younger brother.

Rebel tromps down the stairs with about as much grace as an elephant, more eager to get the night started than to play the role of sophisticated society man. He slips his arm around my waist and curves inward to press a kiss to my neck, a chuckle on his lips. "I saw that," he murmurs, clutching my hip. "And for the record, you have my blessing."

As Thanatos walks away to bring the car around, I grab Rebel's shirt and tug him into my chest. Searching his eyes, I try to puzzle through his thoughts—or, hell, my own. "Everything with you boys is complicated."

He laughs, genuinely sounding happy. "There's

nothing complicated about love, baby." Tracing my lips with his fingertip, he smiles. "Let it in." Kissing me, he licks into my mouth with a contented sigh, like he genuinely believes that adding *another* person into our bed—and our relationship—is a good thing.

For some crazy reason, I might want it, too.

CHAPTER 14

CELIA

AS WE PULL up to the venue, Rebel is high energy, bouncing his knee in the backseat and tapping my knuckles with his fingertips. The moment we've stopped at the curb, he immediately jumps from the vehicle to come around to my side and let me out— "*Like a gentleman,*" he's been insisting for the last half hour.

I have a hard time imagining any of these men as gentleman.

Thanatos catches my reflection in the rearview mirror, his gaze burning into mine. "I'll see you inside, Princess."

"I'm not a princess," I remind him, frowning. "I don't know why you keep calling me that."

"Close enough," he mutters, flicking his gaze to the window.

Ooookay, then.

Just when I think we've made progress with our relationship, Thanatos reminds me that he's as surly as a bear emerging from hibernation. I clench my fists in my lap as flashes of the past few days with him barrage my mind. He's aggressive when he's horny and emotionally detached when he isn't.

Yeah, just like a fucking bear.

My door suddenly snaps open, and the roar of the crowd rushes into the cab. I throw one quick glance at Thanatos to find him staring at me through the rearview again. "You know," I huff, "if you took a page from your brother's book, you might actually enjoy life." Shaking my head, I grab my clutch purse and take a calming breath before accepting Rebel's outstretched hand and allowing him to pull me onto the red carpet.

Flashing lights blind me before I can get a good look at the scene, and I plaster on a winning smile before my vision has cleared. Paparazzi shout in our direction, but Rebel remains calm as he curls his arm possessively around my waist and meets my smile with a dazzling one of his own.

Leaning close, he murmurs in my ear. "Ready for the wolves?"

"It's not these wolves I'm worried about."

We talked through our game plan for the night extensively, going through possible scenarios and how to handle getting separated in a crowd. If we see their father —if we have an opening—we're going to take him out.

Their lone wolf of a father is being hunted—*tonight.*

Rebel's smile glints in the flashing lights, his sharp canines making him appear as wild on the outside as he is within. "You look good with murder in your eyes, baby."

Winking, he pulls me along the walkway even faster, cutting through the meandering guests to enter the venue ahead of our scheduled time. Unlike his brothers, he's eager for the night's festivities—regardless of if that entails watching a team of acrobats swing through the air... or stabbing his father in the throat during the intermission. He'd be thrilled with either outcome.

Although our procession is cut short, I smile toward the cameras and try my best to look the part of the glamorous socialite, despite the butterflies in my gut. In truth, this is my first public appearance since my divorce, and I have not one man accompanying me, but *four*.

That's four distinct chances to make a fool of myself in front of the entire city.

But with Rebel by my side, the odds of public embarrassment dwindle before my eyes. He plays to the camera, knowing exactly how to angle our bodies for the perfect photograph. A hand on my lower back, a whisper in my ear, a gentle brush of his lips across my forehead— nothing is off-limits if it means he can keep touching me *and* maintain the attention of the crowd. More often than not, I catch him staring at me rather than at our destination.

"You don't have to keep doing that," I murmur, meeting his eyes. There's a depth to them that our surroundings can't mask, no matter how loud or chaotic it gets. When he looks at me, sometimes I think he loses focus on everything else and gets caught in the moment.

"Doing what?" he asks, his lips curving into a delicious smirk. A lock of jet-black hair falls into his eyes, making him even more devilishly handsome. Without his lip piercing and tattoos, he could almost pass for a gentleman—if it weren't for the hand hovering dangerously close to my ass.

"Looking at me." I avoid his heavy gaze, my heart squeezing a little too tightly. It's how they all look at me, actually, that throws me off-balance. Rebel's stare is a warm glow that radiates through my body from my head to my toes—leaving no room for a single inch of neglect. The attention is overwhelming, but when we mutually decided to drop our barriers and *do this thing* together... I guess he decided to fall first—and *fast*.

He may not even realize that he's in love.

As Rebel cups my chin and tilts my head up, I part my lips in anticipation of his kiss. Instead, he brushes his thumb across my bottom lip. "You're the best part of my night." He presses a slow kiss to my jawline. "All I want to do—" his lips ghost across my skin as they travel higher—"is look at you." Humming softly, he brushes the tip of his nose against mine, our faces mere inches apart. "Among other things."

My cheeks flush and my heart skips a beat, but it's not from the innuendo. It's from how quickly and easily it is to love him back.

"You believe me, don't you?" There's a subtle hint of vulnerability to his words, like we're not only talking about tonight, but about something bigger than the gala and the gowns.

As his hands wander my waistline, I grab the front of his shirt and pull him closer, our audience be damned.

Even now, when he's dressed to the nines and oozing money, he still smells like leather and smoke. I breathe in his scent, unable to resist.

He smells like home.

"Yes," I whisper, "I do."

His lips linger a mere inch from mine as he groans, clutching at my dress. "Fuck, I love hearing you say that. *Fuck.*" Crashing into me, he steals a kiss that knocks the air from my lungs and tilts my world on its axis. Somewhere in the back of my mind, I'm dimly aware that he's dipped me, bending me backwards with a promise that he'll catch me—hold me—keep me. He grins against my lips as someone in the crowd whistles. We laugh together, breathless and giddy, as he pulls me upright.

"You look fucking amazing in that dress," he rumbles, nipping the shell of my ear as we blindly walk onwards toward the front entrance, the two of us too enraptured in each other to care for the rest of the journey. We skip the photo shoot and step around couples waiting for their glamour shots. "I'm getting hard just looking at you." He laughs, a throaty rasp that catches in his throat. "Damn, baby, gonna have me at half-mast all night."

I join in his laughter, the sound bubbling up like champagne. Light. Fizzy. *Freeing.* Beginning the night with Rebel may have been a tactical move to loosen me up, but I can't fault Rage for it when it's clearly working.

I feel lighter than I have in years.

We finally pass through the high arch leading into a small courtyard where guests can freshen up before checking their coats and handbags. I keep my clutch pinched under my arm as we approach the doors.

"Tickets," an usher wearing a white suit commands, holding his hand out for them. I quickly produce our three remaining tickets for Rebel, Thanatos, and myself and hand them over. "This one will come behind us," I assure the usher, keeping my smile up as I tap Thanatos's ticket with my fingertip.

"All guests have to arrive together," the man drones, already looking behind us at the next approaching guests. "You can wait for him here."

My smile freezes in place while I channel my mother's willpower. Adella Monrovia isn't a woman who is told no—and I'll be damned if I let all of her strict lessons from my childhood go to waste.

A woman has to speak up for herself because no one else will do it for her.

"We'll be going inside now," I tell him, digging the tips of my manicure into his palm. "And you'll let my friend through once he arrives." The ticket crinkles at each point of contact, softening the sting of my fingernails, but the effect is the same as if I'd punctured the man's skin. He stiffens from head to toe and waits for me to remove my hand before attaching Thanatos's ticket to the top of his clipboard. Clearing his throat, he nods towards a security guard a few feet away. "Turn in all electronics and concealed carry weapons, and you can go through."

Rebel makes a show about unclipping a handgun from his waist and turning it in. We discussed this as part of our plan—turn in the most obvious weapons and keep one hidden on your body. Mine is a knife the size of my finger strapped to my thigh, while Rebel has a larger one concealed in the sole of his shoe. I'm not sure what the others are carrying, but after seeing the vast array of options in the weapons locker, I have little doubt that they found something suitable for the evening for each of them.

Once inside the venue, I take a cursory glance around the room, taking in the dozen or so gambling tables set up in the center of the room and the slot machines lining one of the walls. All proceeds for the night are supposed to go to the various charities sponsored by the city's wealthiest elite, but I can hear the clink of poker chips, the tumble of dice, and the raucous laughter that follows from thirty feet away. People are going to get carried away when betting their money, and more than a few of them are going home with fat dollar bills lining their wallets and purses.

It's how the rich like to play—for themselves.

Rebel steers us directly into the fray, landing at the closest gambling table using cards. "Watch me, baby." He licks a stripe across his front teeth and grins. "I'm gonna win you a diamond ring."

My heart stumbles. "A diamond?"

He isn't thinking of *proposing*, is he?

Still grinning, Rebel winks. "Mhm. A diamond ring for my diamond girl. Look at her sparkle, boys!" He waves toward my dress, and I laugh as it dawns on me.

Diamond. Not a wedding ring, but a reference to my

shimmering dress. The dripping stones catch the light with every move I make, making it impossible to blend into the crowd. Although the other women have kept to the event's casino theme, very few of them chose such an eye-catching design, sticking to metallic fabrics and rhinestone bodices in blacks, silvers, or golds. My dress, however, reflects the tiniest specks of light in all directions, catching the eyes of anyone whose mind wanders amidst their conversations.

I lean into Rebel's side and press a quick kiss to his cheek. "Better win for me then, baby." I lift my hand and wiggle my ringless fingers to showcase how empty they are. "Mama needs her sparkle."

A low-pitched moan catches in Rebel's throat. "Yes, ma'am."

While the table plays another round, someone approaches us with a suitcase filled with poker chips lying in neat rows, while his partner supplies a locked cash box. They quickly exchange my date's cash for multiple stacks of chips in red, black, blue, and green, placing all four colors inside a rack for us to carry.

Rebel sets it on the table and claps his hands together as he takes a seat. Glancing at the dealer's name tag, Rebel raps his knuckles on the felt top. "Don't let me down, now, Reggie. You heard my girl—she wants a diamond, so show me a diamond!" After checking the hand he's been dealt, Rebel slides a few chips onto the table to bet on whatever he's looking for as the dealer flips cards over. A neon sign hanging over the table reads *Blackjack* in bright red letters.

My mind wanders as Rebel plays his first game. Where are the others? Is their dad even here? If he isn't, will he show up at all, or are we wasting our time gambling and socializing when we should be out on the streets, as Ruin puts it, "hunting."

Grabbing my hand, Rebel pulls me from my thoughts and into his lap, keeping my back pressed against his chest and his arms wrapped around my waist. "You're my good luck charm," he murmurs, kissing the curve of my neck. "Do you know how to play?"

I shake my head. "I don't really need to know."

Chuffing, he plays with the slit on my dress over my thigh, fingering the seam with one hand while he places a new bet with the other. More cards flip, with one given to each player, and one of the other men at the table curses under his breath as the dealer swipes all three of his cards into a discard stack. Rebel slips his hand beneath my skirt and rubs my bare thigh. "Here, I'll fold this round, and then I'll explain the rules while the next one plays."

Blackjack, as it turns out, is a fast-paced game where winning is determined by chance. Rebel feeds into the chaos, snickering as his opponents "bust" by going over twenty-one points and making them glare in our direction. He pays their animosity no mind, too focused on rubbing his crotch on my ass and tossing chips onto the table. Once he's fully erect, he sighs into my neck and bites down, making me squeal from the sudden burst of pain.

"A lady shouldn't be at the table," an older player gruffs, scowling at us.

My face blooms a deeper shade of pink as I'm stunned into silence. There are beautiful women crawling all over the room—some of whom are stuck wearing skin-tight leotards and tights while serving guests like this guy, for fuck's sake. If this man has a problem with women, he should go to a gentleman-only game in the basement of one of the city's bars, not a VIP charity event.

I grab a glass of amber liquid from a passing server and down the drink in three large swallows, a trickle dripping from the corner of my lips as the alcohol burns my throat. Rebel is quick to lick the spill, a hum buzzing in his chest as he nips my jaw. "Good thing I'm not a lady," I drawl, setting my empty glass down on the table.

"Damn right, you're not," Rebel groans, slipping his hand between my slick thighs. He shivers as his fingertips glide across my heated skin, and I spread my thighs wider for him to feel even more.

The man's gaze narrows before it flickers to the edge of the table covering my body from the waist down. "So you're a whore, then. Guess that means those tits are for sale." With a grunt, he shoves his entire stack of poker chips towards me.

Our dealer shuffles the deck, keeping his eyes glued to the cards as he riffles them between his hands.

I guess the staff is paid to ignore sick fucking bastards if they have enough money.

"Come sit in my lap, sweetheart. I'll show you how a *real* man treats a woman."

The other guests at the table suddenly disperse. Even the dealer, the guy paid to be here, picks up his cards and slips into the crowd, leaving the three of us to handle things ourselves. The back of my neck prickles, and I know that people are watching, likely Rage or Ruin, or maybe even Thanatos. The rest of the crowd ignores us completely, either too caught up in their own world to care or too corrupt to interrupt.

"She's taken," Rebel snaps, wrapping his fist around the knife strapped to my thigh. "Fuck off."

"What, you think because you're some pretty boy, you're too good to share? If she's a whore, then your dick isn't the only one she's sucking tonight—"

Rebel's arm jerks under the table, and the man inhales sharply while his face suddenly reddens, matching the bright neon sign overhead. His lips part, but no sound comes out even as they flop open and closed over and over again. Beads of sweat collect on his forehead as Rebel grins over at him.

"Listen here, fuckface. What I do with my woman is none of your goddamn business." Rebel's arm flexes across my thigh and he twists his wrist in small, circular motions. The muted sound of wet flesh is drowned out by someone winning a jackpot on the slot machines, the screams from the excited winner flooding the air as witnesses clap in celebration.

I grab the holster over my thigh, but I already know that the knife is missing. Keeping my face neutral, I then grab Rebel's wrist to stop him from carving a hole into the man's leg, no matter how small of a hole it would be. I cover my face with my hair and press my lips to Rebel's ear. "We're supposed to be keeping a low profile. Stabbing someone in the leg is *not* keeping a low profile!"

"Neither is fingering you under the table, but some risks are worth it." After stealing a quick kiss, Rebel pulls the knife from the man's leg and slams the sole of his shoe on his chair legs, toppling him over onto his back.

"Rebel!" I hiss, noticing the spark of violence in his eyes for the first time. Is it because that guy called me a whore, or is he itching for a prelim before we meet his father? "We're going to get kicked out!"

He shrugs, nonchalant as ever as he helps me stand, grabs our chips, and laces our fingers together to pull me away from the table. "Worth it."

I follow him to another gambling table, but this time when he sits down, I wrap my arms around his shoulders and lean over the back of his chair, careful to whisper low enough that only he can hear me. "Tonight isn't about us," I remind him, keeping an eye on the security guard that walks over. He hovers near the dealer but keeps his eyes locked on Rebel the entire time.

So much for staying under the radar.

"We're here to keep Ruin alive," I continue, tapping my fingertips against Rebel's chest. Although he keeps his posture loose and his eyes on the game, I can feel his heartbeat quicken when I press my lips to his pulse point. Flicking my tongue against it, I love the way he swallows and fumbles his chip drop, the plastic coin tumbling into an empty cupholder.

"Wash my fucking knife," I growl, "before it ends up in *your* thigh."

Rebel folds his cards immediately and jumps to his feet, squeezing my hand so tightly that it hurts. Leaving all of his chips on the table, he drags me away from the gambling hall and to the bathroom in the back, ignoring the *Men Only* sign as he whisks us inside. Locking the deadbolt on the door, he spins around to face me. "Celia." Advancing slowly, he smirks, a flash of mischief in his eyes. "Did you just threaten to stab me?" He pulls my little knife from his pocket and waves it between us. "Do you know how fucking hot that is? Shit, did they hear it, too?" He fiddles with his earpiece, clicking it on with a muttered curse, then helps me with mine.

I cross my arms over my chest. "That's not the point. You can't lose focus tonight. This is too important."

Rebel's face falls instantly. He tosses the knife into the sink behind him before taking a step closer. "Shit, baby, you're right. You know you're right. I let the game get to me, and that guy—" He clenches his teeth. "—can't fucking call you that. No one can call you that."

"To be fair, I walked into it when I said I wasn't a lady."

"Not the point," he parrots back at me. "But you're right. I need to focus." Grabbing the tent in the front of his pants, he tosses his head back and groans. "Fuck, I'm rock hard."

Rage's voice clicks over our comms. "*Again?* Why the fuck are you hard?"

"Where are you?" It's Ruin speaking this time. "I can't see you."

"We're in the men's room," I sigh, frowning as Rebel rubs the thick outline of his cock. I'd be lying if I didn't admit that I was tempted, but it's like I said. We can't lose focus tonight. "Rebel stabbed someone."

"It's a small knife!"

"It's *my* knife!"

Whining, Rebel hangs his head. "I know, baby, you're right. You should get to stab whoever you want. I'll clean it." He spins around and soaps up the blade, carefully washing the blood and skin off. "Bastard fucking deserved it, though."

Thanatos's voice rumbles across the line. "You two need to cool it. We just got here, and you're already maiming people. Save it for Dad."

"Someone *else* got hurt? Who?"

"Doesn't matter," Rage rumbles.

I bet he's the one who lost his cool. Rolling my eyes, I plant my foot on Rebel's thigh so that he can return my knife to its holster. "Is it time to switch yet?"

"It's a little early, but I think we should. You two did a good job walking inside, but there's too much heat from security. We need to lay low."

Rebel admires my heel for a moment before sliding his palm up my bare calf, taking his time with returning my knife. He leans over and kisses my thigh, sending goosebumps across my skin. "You look way too damn good like this, baby." Carefully, he slips the knife back into its sheath and caresses the leather strap holding it in place. "We've gotta load you up soon. Knives, guns, *fuck*. Can you imagine how that much metal will look on your skin?" He nips the soft flesh on my inner thigh, making my muscles clench. "I can *smell* you from here." Groaning, his eyes flick up to my pussy, begging for a glimpse. "You'll let me fuck you with one, right? Please?"

Someone exhales harshly across the comms. My body ignites, lust pinning me to the spot. "Wh-what?"

Fuck me with *what?*

"*Rebel.*" Rage's voice rumbles like thunder.

A fourth voice joins the conversation, quietly murmuring something that I can barely hear, but I *do* hear it.

We all do.

"*She creamed all over my knife.*"

I gasp, completely mortified. None of them ever mentioned the knife incident with Ruin before, so he must not have told them... until... now...

Rebel grins like the cat who caught the canary. "Oh, baby... did you let Ruin touch you with his knife, after all?" He draws circles on my skin with his thumbs. "That's dangerous. A man could get addicted to something as pretty as that." Addressing Ruin, he continues, "did she take it all the way?"

My body trembles at the memory of Ruin's knife slipping between my thighs, and now, more than ever, I wish I were wearing panties.

I'm *dripping* wet.

The group hangs on Ruin's every word, suddenly aching for the younger man to speak. I hold my breath as I count the seconds, praying that he sticks to his usual method of conversation: grunting. A full minute passes before he exhales, the two of us taking our next breaths together. "She can take more. Her pussy *wants* more. Again and again and again, *krosotka*. All pretty in red tonight." He sucks in another breath, his voice cracking with his next words. "Is she wet, Rebel?" I can hear him lick his lips. "I want a taste."

With a squeak, I bat away Rebel's grabby hands and throw my clutch at his chest. He catches it, grinning wolfishly as I frantically unlock the door behind my back. As much as I'd love for Rebel to go down on me while his brothers can't do anything but listen, if we get side-tracked, the whole plan for tonight goes up in smoke.

But a little teasing... *that* could be fun.

"Don't run away, beautiful. There's nothing to be ashamed of. A little knife play is fun. It's kinky. We like it."

I shake my head and laugh, knowing that all of them can hear me. My fucked-up men, all four of them, even Thanatos. "Maybe I'm not running away," I counter, grinning. "Maybe I'm running *to* something." I blow Rebel a kiss before opening the door and walking backwards through it, loving the way his face lights up.

"Who brought the biggest knife, boys?" I glance around the room, unable to see any of them, but knowing that they can see me. They're always watching, waiting for their turn. "I think it's time for a switch. Any volunteers?"

CHAPTER 15

———

RAGE

I WATCH my woman walk down the red carpet with my brother, the two of them holding their heads high as cameras flash in their direction. Rebel takes the attention in stride, more focused on the woman beneath his arm than the paparazzi. Much like the photographers, he can't take his eyes off of her radiant smile, the gentle curve of his own lips betraying his true feelings for her.

My little brother has fallen in love.

While they wait for the couple preceding them to finish their glamour shots, he tips her chin up and steals a tender kiss, earning shouts and applause from the crowd as they take dozens of photos. A blush dusts Celia's cheeks when their lips part, and she smiles so beautifully that Rebel isn't the only man falling in love.

We all are.

One of the men nursing a scotch beside me at the bar nods toward the approaching couple. "Who is that? The woman." The bartender takes one glance and says Celia's name, likely having been required to memorize every guest on the list of attendees for tonight. When he doesn't elaborate, the guest pulls out his wallet and flashes a twenty-dollar bill. "Tell me more."

I prepared for this exact scenario, anonymously paying the staff to keep tight-lipped about anyone within the bratva's circle, my future wife first and foremost.

Let's see how well this bartender can be bought off.

He stares at the cash for a second before slipping it into the breast pocket of his vest. "There's nothing more to say. She is an esteemed guest for tonight, much like yourself."

The other man slides the bartender a fifty-dollar bill this time. "Bullshit. You know everyone here, Gustav. I know you have some dirt on her pretty little nose."

Gustav the bartender keeps a straight face. "Miss Monrovia is a lovely woman whose charitable contributions over the past decade have helped fund many campaigns. There is no 'dirt' on her nose or elsewhere."

While the two men talk, I shuffle through the guest list in my mind, narrowing down this particular guest's name within a few seconds. Mike Smith, a boring name for a boring man. I down the rest of my drink and slide the glass toward Gustav. Although he's deflecting Mike's questions well, I'd prefer he not say anything at all when it comes to Celia or the other members of my family. I count out a crisp wad of hundred-dollar bills from one of the money clips I had prepared for the evening. Ten should do it. Standing from my seat, I slide the money into Gustav's vest pocket and pat his chest. "Keep her name off your lips for the next week. Ensure that the rest of the staff does the same, and I'll donate tonight's earnings to the tip jar."

With a nod, Gustav refills my glass. "You've got it, boss."

"Who the hell do you think you are?" The man sitting beside me quickly stands, matching my height but not my intensity. "I'm a chairman on this board. I can have you removed from the premises in a heartbeat."

I smile, ensuring to show all of my teeth. "You can try, Mr. Smith, but you know as well as I do that it's a bad idea. I'd hate to show your wife how little authority you have as chairman. It might make her reconsider blowing your tiny dick in the bathroom during intermission. I've heard she's a real good cocksucker. Hate for you to miss it."

Mike Smith's face burns bright red. "What the fuck did you just say about my wife?"

"Only the truth. I have on good authority that she gives a wicked blow job."

He swings a punch that I catch in my fist. "Careful. Breaking hands is a favorite hobby of mine." I squeeze until the man chokes on a squeal. With everything that's been happening lately, I haven't gotten to break any bones. It might do me some good to relieve a little stress on a piece of shit like this.

"Okay, okay! I'll back off!"

What I hate more than anything is a bastard who won't defend his family's honor. "I just called your wife a cocksucker," I snarl, "and you throw *one* punch? Does she mean so little to you?" Slamming his fist onto the counter, I press down hard until his fingers flatten. "Fucking *weak*." I down the rest of my drink before smashing the solid base of my glass into his knuckles, the sickening *crack* of bone music to my ears. He screams as I pound the glass into his flesh, destroying his hand.

Piece of shit husband.

Once I'm satisfied that he'll never be able to grab his dick again, I lean over the counter and drop the bloodied glassware into the sink. "Sorry about the mess," I tell Gustav sincerely. "How much do I owe you?"

Mike Smith has gone pale, the shock over his disfigured hand likely going to his head. I reach into his pocket and produce his wallet, counting the cash inside and handing it all to Gustav. Adding another five hundred from my money clip, I nod. "Don't forget, now. No one says her name."

By the time I've washed the blood from my hands and returned to the ballroom, the cocktails are flowing and the first round of gambling has begun. I missed the introductory speech, but I don't much care for them, anyway, so it's no loss. As I scan the room for Celia, Thanatos weaves through the crowd toward me.

"Should have worn the jacket," I tell him, glancing at his outfit. Rebel can get away with the button up and slacks look, but wearing only a vest and tie? "You look like a server."

"I look like a bouncer," he counters, broadening his stance and clasping his hands in front of him.

"You're not wearing all black. Bouncers wear black."

"I could be undercover."

"You're not. Not for them, anyway."

"They don't know that." He frowns as the guests avoid coming near us, likely sensing the tension rolling off of my older brother in waves. "She seems like she's having a good time."

I glance across the room to find Celia sitting in Rebel's lap. My younger brother presses a kiss to her neck, and a wave of jealousy flares hot inside my chest. I'll have my turn with her tonight, but taking turns is getting old. I'd much rather we all surround her at once to keep the real vultures at bay. I spot them easily, the men searching for someone to take home tonight. A few women, too, from the looks of it. But Rebel is doing a good job of making sure that Celia appears taken.

In hindsight, I should have given her a diamond ring to wear for the evening.

Or forever.

"Yeah, she does." I watch our woman for only a few seconds before tearing my gaze away to check the rest of the room for my youngest brother. I haven't seen Ruin since we first arrived. All it took were a few stares from arriving guests for him to bolt, disappearing before more could gawk at his facial scars. He *says* that he doesn't care what people think, yet he still runs away at the first provocation.

Despite knowing this, I refused to let him bring a mask. What will it say to Celia if she loves him and he never learns to love himself? That she loves something damaged and broken?

I scoff aloud and cross my arms over my chest. There's nothing broken about my brother, and he damn well needs to learn that fact.

It took at least an hour for him to stop gnashing his teeth about walking in here bare-faced. I imagine that he's still brewing somewhere out of sight. "Where is he hiding?" I wonder aloud, scanning the room. "Have you seen him?"

"Who, Ruin?" Thanatos hums in the back of his throat. "Where do you think?" He tilts his head back to stare at the ceiling—or, more accurately, at the intricate catwalk erected over our heads. Although the ballroom is hardly a stage inside a theater, it's treated as one to give the room a Las Vegas vibe. Hundreds of lights beam down at us from above, each one attached to a system of wires and metal bars that criss-cross just beneath the ceiling. It's dark and shadowed above the bulbs, likely for effect more than anything. I'm sure as the night wares on, they'll dim the lights so it looks like we're standing beneath a night sky.

If Ruin is hiding somewhere, it's up there in the rafters, like he's a character from the *Phantom of the Opera* or some shit. He's always had a flare for the dramatic. I'm sure he gets it from Rebel, the two of them feeding off of each other's energy.

The tech crew will have access to the scaffolds and catwalk, but I have no doubt that Ruin has found his way up there, too. He's probably smoking, too, staring down his nose at the festivities from high up above, no doubt keeping an eye out for our father as much as he is for Celia. When it's his turn in the rotation, I imagine that he'll carry her up there just to watch her reaction to the height and heat.

I bet it's sweltering up there.

"He should go last," I muse, sighing. "He'll ruin her hair and makeup." Not to mention her dress and shoes. The pair cost us a fortune, taking out most of Rebel's winnings from a few nights ago. If her dress tears, someone will start a rumor that she was having sex in the bathrooms and that her lover got too rough when he lifted her dress. These parties always attract the juiciest gossip on account of how much time the clientele have on their hands.

Then again, with how uptight Than looks right now, he might need to be the start of a dirty rumor.

"Why don't you go next," I tell him, relinquishing my spot as Celia's second date for the night. My fist clenches as soon as the words pass my lips, but I won't take them back. Than needs to loosen up, or he'll be a perpetual stick in the mud for the rest of our lives.

I know that he likes her. They could even be friends. He's just too goddamn stubborn to admit it.

Rather than look relieved, Thanatos damn near panics. "I don't want that. I don't need a turn at all. I'm not here to party." He twitches, shifting his weight from foot to foot and showing a nervous tic that I've never seen before.

He won't look me in the eye.

"Are you scared of her?" Lifting an eyebrow, I study his reaction. It's not like him to have anxiety. "Or is this about Dad? Celia made a good point the other night. He probably won't show up without an invite."

Good thing that Ruin and I left the bastard notes all over town. For the past week, any back alley he could have walked through had his initials painted in blood red, with a safety deposit box number that matches our old home address directly beneath it. We rented out every single box in the city with that number and placed a personal invitation to tonight's gala inside.

If our father was waiting for an invitation, he finally has one.

I should have let Thanatos in on the secret, but if he knew that our father were *actually* coming, I never would have gotten him to agree to attend as a guest. Instead, he'd be perched up above in a makeshift sniper nest, scoping out the event. Although that would have come in handy when our father shows his face, we owe Ruin the kill. Thanatos would pull the trigger a dozen times before our brother could ever get close.

For that reason, I need Thanatos on the ground tonight.

But I also need him to make up with Celia and put water under the bridge. They've had their differences— he gave a shit apology—and they've been getting along better ever since their training started. I can see the tension between them softening more with each passing day. By the time the baby comes, however, I need them to be a rock solid unit like the rest of us. If I go down for any reason, I need someone responsible to be there to take care of her when I'm gone. I can't count on Ruin to change diapers, and I sure as shit can't count on Rebel to make our kid lunch before school. A nanny would help, but I doubt Celia wants one if it means taking away quality time with her child, and I'm not letting Adella fucking Monrovia anywhere near our family, no matter how much we might need the help.

That leaves someone like our bratva queen Valentina Baranova taking position as auntie, but for a fatherly role...

I need Thanatos.

Which means that he and Celia need to start bonding ASAP.

That can't happen if Than is preoccupied with something else. Our father is an easy problem to solve when you get down to the brass tacks of the situation, so I doubt Than is anxious about committing patricide. Which leaves only one other possibility...

"I've never known you to be scared of anything," I admit slowly, watching Than to check for cracks in his armor. They're starting to show. "Tell me, then, what is it about Celia that's got you tied up in knots, brother?"

Thanatos stares out at the sea of people before answering my question. He doesn't seem surprised that I'm asking, which means that he's been pondering that same thing. "She's good for you."

I wait a second before responding. "She's good for all of us."

He keeps his expression neutral, hiding something from me. If I had to guess, it's that he feels guilty—either for not liking her, as he vehemently expressed when they first met at the safe house in The Backyard, or...

For liking her too much.

Until he tells me the truth, I won't mention my suspicions. He could flee the minute our father is out of the picture, and that's the last thing I want. We've already been separated for all the years he wasted chasing our father down; Thanatos deserves more than a life on the road, hunting his next kill.

He deserves a family—and I intend to give him one.

"You're going next," I unilaterally decide. "Give Rebel another hour with her, and then I want you to sweep her off her feet."

Thanatos's eyes narrow. "You can't be serious."

My lips curve into a smirk. "I'm dead serious. I want her to have a good time tonight. I want *you* to have a good time. What better way to ensure that happens than by putting two of my favorite people together?"

And if rumors fly, so fucking be it.

We've got the rest of our lives to prove them wrong.

"What is he *doing*?" Thanatos scowls in the distance, clearly ignoring my generous gift of giving him Celia early. It's a damn kind gesture from the depths of my heart. A valiant effort to patch our family's holes, and he's not even interested enough to entertain the idea?

My mood dips, and I clench my jaw to keep from rescinding the offer. He *needs* to spend time with Celia, and this is the easiest way to force him into it. Forcing myself to breathe, I follow Than's gaze across the room to where Rebel and Celia are sitting. Knowing my brother, he's either flirting too hard or pissing someone off. "He's probably just—"

Picking a fight.

As the man sitting opposite them topples over in his chair, Rebel pulls Celia to her feet, and the pair drifts off to another game table to claim a new seat. The man they've left behind on the ground clutches his leg in agony, a few guests standing around gawking while a bouncer and a paramedic rush in. Another man follows Rebel to the new table, clearly hired muscle for the event.

"Rebel," I growl, knowing he can hear me through our earpieces. "What the fuck did you do?"

"Looks like a stab wound," Thanatos grumbles, scowling. "I didn't see him pull a knife, though."

"It was under the table. *Rebel.* Fucking answer me."

Neither he nor Celia pick up. "Fucker left his comms off, too."

I'm not surprised that he would forget to turn it on in favor of turning *her* on. Closing my eyes, I take a deep breath and count to ten. "He's going to get us in trouble."

Thanatos lifts an eyebrow. "Are you forgetting about your little stunt at the bar?" After a moment, he sighs. "This mission was doomed before we ever started. None of you can keep your cool." His face twists, pulling at the scar on his lips. "I'll have to take him out myself."

"Because *that* went so well before." I can't help but be an asshole when I'm in a bad mood. "You had years to take him out, Than. Why couldn't you?"

"I shot him," he grumbles, "but the bastard didn't

die. Hobbled away and went underground. There's only so much I can do without bratva resources behind me, Rage." He scowls at me. "In case you've forgotten, when I left, I was exiled. I ran into old teammates on the road, and they pretended I didn't exist. Completely ignored me in fear of the consequences."

"That was Tolkotsky's era, not Andrei's." It's ominous to speak our old *pakhan*'s name, but the bastard is dead and buried. "For what it's worth, you were dealt a shit hand. I know you left for good reason, and I don't fault you for it." I jab my fist against his chest. "But this shit right here? Stop doubting it. We'll kill him —together."

"*Tonight*," he vows, nodding. "Yeah. Okay."

We watch as Rebel and Celia get up from their table *again* and quickly disappear into the men's restroom. After a moment, Celia's voice fills my ear.

"That's not the point. You can't lose focus tonight. This is too important."

"Damn right it is," I mutter, sighing. As we listen to their conversation, I study Thanatos's face. He takes a drink from a passing server and leans against a support beam for the monstrous city of lights over our heads. Ruin must be listening and lurking, too, all of us hanging on Rebel and Celia's every word.

They're arguing.

It's short-lived, however, with Rebel groaning that he's *rock hard.*

"Again?" I snap. "Why the fuck are you hard?"

Thanatos's mouth presses into a thin line as he swirls the drink in his hand without taking a sip.

Ruin's voice suddenly joins the conversation. "Where are you? I can't see you."

"We're in the men's room. Rebel stabbed someone."

"Called it," Than grunts. Then, louder, "You two need to cool it. We just got here, and you're already maiming people. Save it for Dad."

"Someone *else* got hurt? Who?"

I pinch the bridge of my nose. Fucking galas—always a mess. "Doesn't matter." Mike Smith will keep his mouth shut if he knows what's good for him.

Celia asks if we should switch, and I think it's a damn fine idea. I'm about to suggest that Thanatos go next when Rebel starts talking again, muttering about how good Celia looks with a weapon, until finally, he says something that catches all of our attention.

"You'll let me fuck you with one, right? Please?"

I clench my fists by my sides. I need a fucking drink for this conversation. "*Rebel.*"

Softer than the rest of them, Ruin's voice suddenly whispers in our ears. "She creamed all over my knife."

Thanatos's eyes damn near bug out of his skull. My ears ring as I process the image burning into my mind: Celia lying on her back, completely naked, while my little brother spreads her legs with the tip of his knife. Then what? When was this?

Rebel's voice rasps in my ear, sounding as turned on as I feel inside. "Did she take it all the way?"

Fuck. Than is right—we're all distracted. *Way too goddamn distracted.*

But so is Thanatos—a vein in his neck throbs in time with his jackhammer heartbeat, and he's about to crush the glass in his hands. I pull it away from him and down the entire drink in one swallow, feeling the burn all the way to my soul. We're sinners for wanting to see our girl with a knife in her pussy. Depraved. Savages.

Then Ruin slams the nail in the coffin for all of us. "She can take more. Her pussy *wants* more." His voice cracks as he asks Rebel if she's wet. "I want a taste," he admits softly.

My throat clicks on a swallow. So do I, brother.

Judging from the way Thanatos licks his lips, I'm thinking that he does, too.

Can I share her with *another* man, though? I grit my teeth as I fight wave after wave of possessive fury roaring in my veins. It's hard enough sharing her with Rebel and Ruin—adding Thanatos to the roster just might kill me. That's four men vying for her attention—when all I want is her eyes on me. Haven't I sacrificed enough for this family? Or do I have one more in me?

Rebel's voice derails my train of thought. "Don't run away, beautiful. There's nothing to be ashamed of. A little knife play is fun. It's kinky. We like it."

Yeah, we like it a lot.

"Maybe I'm not running away," Celia counters lightly. "Maybe I'm running *to* something. Who brought the biggest knife, boys?"

Thanatos crumples, bending at the waist like he's

been stabbed in the heart. I snicker, knowing that he brought a gun to a knife fight. *Shit*, but so did I. The one time that a gun loses that battle *has* to be tonight?

Celia emerges from the men's room, a bounce in her step and a smile beaming across her face. She blows Rebel a kiss before turning to the room—and the three men ravenous for her wet fucking pussy to sit on our faces.

"I think it's time for a switch. Any volunteers?"

There's a flicker of light from above, and I can hear thudding footsteps through our comms. I scoff, knowing that if it's a fight between Rebel and Ruin to snatch Celia up, even if Rebel has a head start, Ruin's going to win. He'll pluck her from the crowd like a daisy from a meadow—without anyone noticing that she's gone missing.

"Tough luck," I tell Thanatos, clapping his shoulder. "You'll still get your turn tonight, just not next."

It looks like Ruin has the honor of stretching our girl's pretty pussy with his knife—and to be honest, I wouldn't have it any other way.

CHAPTER 16

CELIA

I RUSH through the throng of guests crowding around poker tables, cocktail stations, and sitting areas, recognizing more than a few faces but too preoccupied to smile or wave or pretend that I'm here to socialize.

My heart leaps to my throat as I weave in and out of bodies, my sparkling heels clicking loudly with each step I take. Off-white marble floors and columns give the opulent hall an appearance similar to Cesar's Palace in Vegas, and as I dart around tables laden with donations for this evening's silent auction, I can't help but laugh. I've never left the city, yet my life feels a thousand times different than it did a year ago. Six months ago. *One month ago.*

Life can change in the blink of an eye.

I used to hate that about the world—that one second, you can be breathlessly happy and in love, and the next you can be crumpled on the floor, crying your heart out. It's cruel to have such heavy doses of whiplash, each one failing to numb us for the next blow. They keep coming, one after the other, until either your body or your heart gives out.

Not long ago, I thought I was ready to carve out the bloody, aching lump of flesh in my chest and offer it to whichever god or demon would put me out of my misery... and then everything began to change. Things weren't exactly *better*, not at first, but they were *less*.

Less painful.

Less broken.

Less difficult.

One day at a time, each breath in my lungs got easier to hold without feeling like my ribs were on the verge of collapse. Ruin and I haven't talked about the pain of his adolescence or the scars carving through his flesh and bone, but I imagine that for him, it's the same.

Excruciating at first, and then... slowly, things feel better.

It's a drastic simplification of a long, drawn-out process that I'm sure is hell on the body and mind, but it's something I can understand in my own way. "I want to understand," I mutter to myself, peering around a large column near the hors d'oeuvres. My gaze travels up the massive column to find that the usual domed ceiling has been replaced with metal beams and countless lights spilling a hazy orange glow across the entire ballroom. Doors leading into adjacent ballrooms separate various events for the evening, the closest of them being an acrobatic show starting at midnight.

There are at least five hours before midnight, so I

have plenty of time to wander... and avoid a certain man or two hunting me down.

"Celiaaa," Rebel purrs in my earpiece, "you really shouldn't run if you want me to take tonight seriously." He chuckles, and another, deeper voice joins in, signaling that at least two of my men are enjoying the latest turn of events.

Playing hide and seek wasn't part of our plan.

"That's the *opposite* of what you should do," he continues. "I'm not gonna look for anyone but you now."

Well, at least Rebel's consistent.

One of his brothers scoffs, but I can't tell which one.

"What about your dad?"

Rage cuts in. "Yes, Rebel, what about Dad, hm? Did you forget about the reason we're fucking here?"

"Fuck 'im." Rebel laughs, the sound dancing across my ribs as I inhale. "But I'd rather fuck you, baby, so c'mere. I promise, we can go where no one will see us."

I check the lock on a plain white door that blends into the wall, the label across it reading *EMPLOYEES ONLY*. It opens without a hitch, making my nerves skitter down my arms like skipping stones across a lake. I don't break rules. I don't trespass. I don't do anything remotely out of line...

But it's like I told the asshole at the blackjack table; tonight, I'm not a lady.

I'm the bait.

"We can't," I tell Rebel, careful to time pushing the door open as a wave of servers carrying drink trays passes by. I quickly slip through the crack and into the room ahead, temporarily blinded by the sudden shift from light to dark.

The room is pitch black aside from glow-in-the-dark gaffer tape outlining a path going straight, left, or right. I reach out to touch the wall in front of me, but my hand falls through the open air. I wave my arms around, looking for a wall or a light switch, and find none. This section of the room must be open, then. But how do I turn on the lights?

"Oral, then," Rebel continues, the clink of metal coins in the background letting me know that he's near the slot machines. "Unless you were hoping for my knife?" He groans loudly. "Fuck, baby, please tell me that you want the knife. I *know* you do. Ruin said—"

"We know what he said," Rage growls, "so stop fucking around. *Krosotka*, you shouldn't be alone."

"The plan was to let me wander around in between our dates so that I would be vulnerable to ambush." Rage can't be angry that I'm sticking to the plan we strategically laid out in case his father showed up tonight. "I'm just sticking to protocol."

"Fuck the protocol." Rage exhales harshly, crackling his mic. "I'm coming to get you."

"You don't have a knife," I point out, taking careful steps down a strip of glow-in-the-dark tape. "Do you, Rage?"

Another deep chuckle rumbles in my ear. I can almost hear it in the air around me, filling the empty shadows. My fingertips brush against a thick rope dangling from up above, the spiraling threads woven tightly and smooth to the touch. I've never been to the circus or any of the traveling shows that roll through the city, so I don't actually know how acrobats swing through the air, if at all. What could the rope be for?

I squint in the dark, but I can barely make out shapes five feet in front of me, let alone up in the air. Shuffling forward, I stumble as my heel catches on a cord, and I tumble into a set of cold metal bars.

Blue and purple lights click on overhead, but only in the highest peaks of the room, bathing the ground floor in pale, silvery light. I lift one of my heels and twist it in the light, watching the starburst shimmers with a smile on my lips. The deep reds of my dress soften into a dusty magenta, each sparkling dewdrop casting a faint glow around my body.

I'm impossible to miss in a room full of shadows.

...and I'm alone. *I think.*

But then who turned on the lights?

A figure steps out from the shadows across the room, walking into the false moonlight to reveal himself. I hold my breath as the man comes into focus, my heartbeat fluttering beneath my ribs. "Rage," I breathe, reaching for the knife hidden beneath my skirt, "I'm—I'm not alone."

"What? Where are you?"

The man lifts a finger to his lips, and it's only then that I catch the discoloration on his hands—ones that I've come to know very intimately over the past few weeks. "I'm okay,"

I assure Rage, adrenaline tripping through my system. "I promise." Reaching up to my ear, I click off my comms and stare at my masked man—only tonight, he isn't hiding.

Not from me. Not anymore.

Dark hair sticks to his forehead and neck, wildly blown around like he's been caught in a windstorm. One small bandage sticks to the curve of his neck, but the rest are missing, leaving his skin bare. He walks across the plush mat covering the floor between us, stopping once he reaches the center. His scars glow in the low light, their color and shape shifting as he moves. "Come here, *krosotka.*"

Something silver flashes in his hand.

A large hunting knife.

The same one he touched me with before.

I swallow hard, knowing that I asked for this. I teased Rebel and ran away, only to find his brother lying in wait. Rebel would have been gentle, coaxing an orgasm from my body with his tongue.

I don't know what to expect from Ruin, and that's what scares me.

"You're trembling." Tilting his head to the side, Ruin studies me. "Are you scared?"

"Yes."

He grunts, pointing the tip of his knife up and tapping it against his bare shoulder. His white dress shirt is carelessly slung over his torso, barely holding on with the few buttons at the bottom. The suit jacket and tie I picked out for him are long gone, lost to the night. But it's not his clothing that captivates me—it's his glowing eyes, the way they never blink.

It's like he won't let go of a single moment.

Slowly, I walk the short distance and come to a stop directly in front of him. Tiny bursts of light reflect off of my dress and heels, and he reaches out to roll a bead between his fingertips.

"You're glowing."

As he stares at my dress, I stare at him. The scars on his body are multi-layered, the old mixing with the new. Some of the wounds are barely healed, his flesh still mending, but he doesn't flinch away from my gaze.

Nor does he flinch away from my touch.

I trace a bruise on his ribs, my hand shaking. His body is hot to the touch—breathlessly warm and inviting—and I lay my palm flat over his heart to feel its beat.

Steady and slow.

"You're calm," I murmur, chuckling at how different we are. "How can you be calm right now?"

Ruin grunts, taking a step closer. "You calm the voices, *krosotka*." He lifts the knife higher and taps the sharp tip against the side of his head. "I can still hear them screaming. The echoes." His heartbeat picks up as his gaze drifts inward, but only for a moment. It settles in an instant, his focus returning. He twists the bead between his fingers until the thread snaps and it slips into his palm.

Braving a glimpse inside his head, I murmur, "what echoes? Whose?"

He doesn't answer, tugging another bead off of my

dress instead. They slip through his fingers and tumble to the mat, bouncing at our feet. "I think they haunt me." Exhaling slowly, he lifts his gaze to mine. "But I don't think they'll touch you." With a tug at the side of my dress, he undoes the zipper and tugs it down. My top loosens, and I gasp as Ruin palms my ribs, counting the rungs under his breath. He tugs the dress down my body until it pools at my feet, then continues his silent exploration of my body. When one hand isn't enough, he grabs my hand and curls my fingers around his knife hilt.

Our eyes meet, and he takes a deep breath as he lets go.

While he touches every inch of my skin, from the tender spot behind my knees to the points of my elbows, I stand perfectly still, unsure what to do. Goosebumps trail down my arms, traveling across my chest and stomach, then down my thighs. Ruin pauses to inspect my pebbled skin, then leans in to press a kiss above my belly button.

I inhale sharply as he continues, dragging his lips from hip to hip, then lower, dropping to his knees to kneel before me. Slowly, he pushes my feet farther apart, forcing me to widen my stance. I tremble as he stares between my thighs, his breath soft as he leans closer.

He kisses my mound, then arches his back and dips lower, slipping his tongue between my lips to taste my desire. Hooking his hands over my calves, he holds me still as I twitch and soft cries fall from my lips. What he lacks in experience he makes up for in patience, taking his time lapping at my folds and flattening his tongue over my clit to feel every quiver and shake of my body. His hands travel higher, rubbing my inner thighs before pulling my labia apart and granting him deeper access.

I damn near drop the knife as he pushes one thick finger inside my pussy. Frantically, I push him back and kick off my heels, growing desperate for more.

While I tear at his shirt and toss it to the floor, he undoes his belt and pulls his pants below his hips, his erection springing free. A bead of precum leaks from the tip. Sitting back on his haunches as I step out of my dress and kick it away, he peers up at me, a small smile curving on his lips as I take small, shaking steps toward him.

My heart stutters as I drop into his lap and curl my arms around his neck, careful to hold the knife out from our bodies. He reaches up and grabs my hand. "Hold it," he rasps, pulling the blade lower, "here." He presses its sharp edge to the side of his neck and closes his eyes, his nostrils flaring as he exhales slowly and tension slips from his shoulders.

Panic beats its wings inside my chest. "Ruin, I can't—"

His eyes snap open, and the smile falls from his lips. "Hold it."

"I could hurt you really badly—"

"*Hold it.*" His eyes flash silver as he grabs my hips. "Do *not* let go." Dragging my body over his, he presses my core to his hard length and thrusts, hissing through his teeth as his cock slides between my lips. We moan in unison as he drags through my slick folds, but it's me who cries out as he punches up and bumps my clit, sending sparks of heat deep into my belly.

The knife slips on his next thrust, cutting into his skin. He groans, pushing my hips down until the tip of his cock slips inside. As crimson blood drips down the knife and the side of his neck, his cock jerks, spilling his seed. Adrenaline courses through my veins as I drop the knife and apply pressure to the wound, wrapping my hand around his neck and squeezing.

As he draws a lungful of air, he grabs my wrist and pries it from his neck. The cut isn't deep, but it's long, spanning a few inches. When he swallows, blood flows faster, trailing down his neck and pooling in the dip of his collarbone. "Pick it up," he rumbles, staring into my eyes. "*Pick it up, krosotka.*"

He doesn't let go until I've put the knife back to his neck. Seemingly satisfied, he brushes the tip of his nose against the column of my throat and sighs. "I am not like my brothers," he says after a moment. His teeth scrape my pulse point, with his tongue quickly following the same path. "I can't give you the same things. I'm..." Shivering, he presses a gentle kiss to my carotid artery. "Haunted." Lifting his face to mine, he stares deeply into my eyes, his gaze pinging back and forth between them. "But you are not," he muses, sighing against my lips. "Your soul is bright, *krosotka*. Mine is..." He purses his lips. "Ash."

"Hey," I breathe, careful not to move the knife again, "hey, I don't believe that."

Humming in the back of his throat, he taps his

fingertips against the side of my ribs. "We're all trapped in cages. Your heart and mine. Forced to keep beating, because no one can reach it." He hooks his fingers, digging into my flesh hard enough to hurt. I wince, and he stops, grunting. "I can cut it out. Make the pain go away. I've done it before, with the others." Wrapping his arms around me, he holds me close, enveloping me in the warmth of his body. I pull the knife away just in time to avoid causing more damage, but this time, he doesn't tell me to put it back. He buries his face in my hair and inhales, shuddering. Quietly, he mutters, "I don't want you to haunt me. I want your soul to stay next to mine."

I carefully set the knife down on the floor and reach for Ruin's hand, lacing our fingers together. His blood sticks to our skin, fusing our palms. With my other hand, I press down on his throat and push him back a few inches, keeping my thumb over the deepest part of the cut. Thankfully, I didn't hit anything major, but it was close.

Really close.

"I'm not going anywhere," I assure him. "My soul is staying right here next to my heart."

"Next to mine," Ruin whispers, his eyes swirling like pools of molten silver.

Lifting myself higher on my knees, I brush my lips over his. "Next to yours. Just like this." Gently, I press my mouth to his, like we've done a few times before. It takes him a moment to react, like he's still unsure about this part, but that's okay with me. I already have two over-bearing kissers—I don't need a third.

We kiss slowly, taking our time to explore our connection. I kiss the corner of his mouth over his scars, and he shivers but doesn't pull away, letting me slide my tongue across his lips. I sigh into his mouth when he lets me in, and I'm the one to deepen the kiss, clutching his throat as I push him down onto his back. The knife lay forgotten by his side as I lay on top of him, long locks of my hair falling over my shoulder, the ends tickling his chest. He wraps his hand in the strands and pulls, getting blood in my hair as he drags me down for another kiss.

A *harder* one.

Our teeth knock together, and I smile, giddy with excitement and nerves and what little adrenaline remains in my system. Ruin grunts as his cock slides out of my pussy, his body shuddering beneath mine and his breaths ragged.

It must still be sensitive.

I wonder if he's ever been with a woman before, but then I remember all the times that Rebel has shown Ruin what to do, and I realize that I'm probably his first. If the kissing wasn't a give away, then the way he looks at me is.

Wide, owl eyes, and a look of wonder that makes me blush. He brushes his knuckles across my rosy cheek, then lowers them to my matching nipple. As his gaze shifts between the two, I study his face, then carefully press my lips to his forehead.

"Let's get you bandaged up, okay?" I scan his body for injuries, but although his burns look fresh and the new skin even fresher, he doesn't complain as I prod him with two of my fingertips, like the medic Serena taught me while we were at The Box. Ruin lets me poke and press his abdomen, his ribs, everywhere that should hurt.

"I told you before," he muses, a soft smile curving on his lips. "You won't find one." He touches the wound on his neck and grunts. "I have no weak spots, *krosotka.*"

"Hm." I stare into his dark eyes and try not to say what's on my mind... because if he learns that loving someone is a weakness...

Well, he won't have *zero* weak spots anymore.

He'll have four... just like the rest of us.

CHAPTER 17

RUIN

FOR AS LONG AS I can remember, my body has always felt tight. Like I'm a snake trying to shed my skin, but I can't scratch enough, bleed enough, hurt enough to break free. Stuck in a perpetual cycle of discomfort with little to ease the tension.

When the pressure builds into a constant buzz in my skull, there are few things that help.

Killing is one of them. Ripping through muscle and sinew is more therapeutic than five hours in the gym with Rage or smoking on the rooftop with Rebel. It's the final moment when the soul leaves the body—the ultimate transcendence—that eases the tension the most.

I've always thought that witnessing Celia's own transcendence into the ether would be the ultimate gift, the one thing that would finally ease the tension racking my bones... and yet, somehow *this* is better than anything I ever imagined.

The weight of Celia's body on mine is a balm to my

frayed nerves—a full-bodied relief that calms the steady ache in my bones. Air rushes from my lungs and she breathes it in, our bodies moving to the rhythm of our hearts, of our souls.

Hers is shining like a lantern in the dead of night, guiding me with each flicker of its warmth, coaxing me closer, until finally, our two souls collide.

My body slips inside of hers and the heat building in my core suddenly bursts, my cock jerking like a loaded gun finally emptying its chamber. I drag in thick lungfuls of air, but all I can taste is the precious salt of her skin and the heavy earth of her body, dragging me underground.

Rebel has always described sex as this burning, aching need; a desire whose thirst can never be quenched.

But as Celia's lips fall over mine, crashing like ocean waves against the shore, meeting me stroke for slick stroke, I find that it's the opposite.

Cool and dark, damp and soft. Everything I crave.

Her lips touch mine, and I forget how to breathe. I don't want to—content to stay in the darkness for as long as her body is curled around mine, our souls mingling while our hearts drum to a shared beat. As Celia pushes me onto my back and straddles my waist, the edges of my vision fade out of focus until all I can see, all I can feel, is her body touching mine. I'm bleeding— my favorite knife having kissed my own skin—and Celia cares more than I do, constantly trying to stem the flow. Once she finally relents, I dirty her body, painting her palm and then weaving my crimson fingers through her hair, pulling her down, down, down—back beneath the cool earth, where everything is better.

With her.

Just the two of us.

She seems to think that our time is limited, muttering something about bandaging my wounds and reaching for her dress. I grab her wrist, determined to keep her. "No." Her face turns toward me, and I pull her in for another taste, repeating the word against her lips. *No.*

We're not leaving yet.

Quickly fixing my button and belt, I shove my dick back inside my pants and I lift Celia off the ground, anchoring her to my hips and sprinting to the back of the room. She latches onto my body, her legs wrapping around my waist and her arms clinging to my shoulders. I breathe in the salt of her skin, licking her neck with a groan.

I don't know how I've lived without tasting her.

"Where are we going?" She lifts her head to look around, but the room is still dark. She won't be able to guess our destination until we're there.

And then it will be too late to run.

The best thing about gaining someone's trust is that breaking it becomes as easy as breaking someone's finger. They hold out their hand for you to take, and you snap their digits at the knuckle before they realize the danger they're in. The shock. The screams. The fear.

A shiver rolls down my spine as I carry Celia up the stairs hidden behind the raised platform. I'm sure that the gymnasts occupying this space for the show tonight have a playbook for both entertainment and safety, keeping within the confines of each so that no one in the audience or their troupe gets hurt, but until they arrive, this place—in all its darkness and vast emptiness—is *mine*.

Just like Celia.

We make it to the top of the platform, and she's still holding onto me, the unsteady trill of her heartbeat making me smile. "Close your eyes," I instruct, waiting to approach the ledge until she obeys. I peer over the edge at the safety net hanging below, knowing that the two-story drop will scare most people—Celia likely included. It's tempting to throw her over without warning, but I want to see the spark of fear in her eyes up close.

Carefully setting her down onto her bare feet, I keep one arm wrapped around her waist as I reach for a silk strand hanging from a metal bar nearby. There are multiple colors to choose from, but I grab the closest one without caring for the aesthetic.

Just seeing Celia bound at the wrists will be pleasurable enough.

"Hold still." I take her wrists in my hands and bring them together at the front, quickly wrapping them in the silk and tying a tight knot. It's not as pretty as rope, but it does the trick, sending a shiver of anticipation down my spine. I've always pictured Celia bound by pretty red rope as I watch her sleep in that fluffy white bed of hers, both of our desires satiated while she sleeps.

I know that she craves safety and stability after her ex-husband's mistreatment, and my brothers want to give that to her. She'll be satisfied while in a relationship with them. My wants, however, will expand her desires until we want the same thing.

To covet one another—completely, irrevocably, *permanently.*

I want her brand on my soul as much as I want mine on hers.

"Ruin?" Her voice is a tight, little whisper of doubt. "What, um, what are you doing?"

With one hand holding her bound wrists and the other brushing the curtain of hair off of her face, I press my forehead to hers and close my eyes, exhaling every ounce of air from my lungs. I hold my breath and count my heartbeats for a long moment, enjoying the silence surrounding us. It's peaceful up here, more so than hovering over the casino next door was. I speak without replenishing my oxygen, scraping my voice across her skin. "Taking. And giving." My next breath pulses in my veins, and I release it across her rosy cheek. "I'm giving you everything, *krosotka.*"

Everything that I know to give.

She opens her eyes and stares into mine, the brush of her breath on my lips a gift that I greedily take, inhaling as deeply as I can. Then she looks around, taking in our location and tilting her head back to stare up at the ceiling—not nearly so far away as from down below on the mat. The pale light shines in her eyes, the glow of color matching the lavender silk tied to her wrists. "What —" She swallows and starts again. "What are we doing up here? Isn't it dangerous?"

The lilt of fear in her voice is the sweetest music to my ears.

I carefully wrap the tail of silk around her waist and over her hips, cutting between her thighs and spiraling around each one before tying another knot around her ankles. She stands perfectly still for me, resting her bound wrists across my shoulders as kneel at her feet. The silk slides across her skin as perfectly as her dress does —*better*, even, digging into her flesh so that it bulges around the banding. I press a kiss to the sides of her calves, then to the tips of her kneecaps, up her plush thighs and over her soft stomach. As I stand, I cup her breast in my hand and squeeze, enjoying the pucker of her nipple and the goosebumps that surround it. When I bend to kiss her there, she gasps, trembling as I wrap my lips around the stiff bud and swirl my tongue over it. She keens low, the sound catching in the back of her throat.

My *krosotka* can do better than that.

Pinching her nipple between my teeth then sucking hard, I groan at the breathless way she moans, her back arching and pushing her breast into my mouth. I open my jaw wider, taking more of her flesh between my teeth, and *bite*. Hard. Bruising her skin, groaning at the thought of marking her pretty body, grabbing her hips to keep her steady as she squeals, high-pitched and panicked. The sound echoes in the chamber and rever-berates inside my ribcage, finding its home wrapped around my heart.

"R-Ruin!" Her breathless cries spur me on, and after lathing the bite mark with my tongue, I latch onto her other breast and do the same, closer to the nipple, catching the tip with my teeth as I pull back to admire her purpling skin. My marks. My cries. My body.

Mine.

I trail my lips along her collarbone, then tip up to kiss the long column of her throat, enjoying the vibrations of her voice on my tongue. I drag in a breath and moan with her, my cock suddenly rock hard and aching all over again, like it can't get enough of her.

My heart agrees, pumping hard and fast.

"*Krosotka*," I rasp, grabbing her ass and squeezing, "you'll look so pretty when you fly." I press an open-mouthed kiss to her forehead then dip to claim her mouth, drowning in desire for this woman. I want so many things from her, and I don't know how to keep up with the rapid-fire pace of them shocking my system. *Bang, bang, bang*—like a clip emptying into my chest, burrowing each new idea into my heart and soul. For now, I want to taste this moment—hear the way she sounds falling through the air, unable to catch herself, unable to *breathe*—

I test our connection by pushing her a little, teetering her over the edge. She gasps and leans her weight forward into me, but without use of her hands or feet, she bends like a rag doll to my will. I hold her out at arm's length as she scrambles for purchase, trying in vain to latch onto the platform with her toes.

"Wait, wait, wait! Don't do this! Ruin, *please!*" Her eyes widen beautifully, the flush across her cheeks paling with her sudden alarm.

"What's wrong, *krosotka*?" I grip the silk knot between her wrists as tightly as I can, knowing that this is the final moment before I let go. "I'm right here with you."

I will always be with you.

With one final push, she falls like an angel from the heavens, her body wrapped in the prettiest silk but a devil's touch marring her skin, marking her as mine.

Forever *mine*.

CHAPTER 18

THANATOS

CELIA'S SCREAM echoes as she falls from a platform two stories high, my heart leaping to my throat at the way her body drops like a stone. My youngest brother stands at the top, shirtless and damn near glowing in the gentle spotlight, his skin pale despite the scars on his body. If I didn't know any better, I'd say that he was Lucifer himself, already having rended the wings from his flesh and cast them aside, now watching his chosen prey fall from grace, damned by his touch.

I don't wish ill will on any of my brothers, but there's a layer of hell made for men like us—especially for a man like Ruin.

Tormenting girls just to hear them scream *can't* be a kink that goes unpunished, especially when she pleaded with his name on her lips.

Ruin, please!

I clench my eyes shut and shake her voice from my head, knowing that it will join the rest of the sounds catalogued in my brain. The bubble of her laughter. The gut-wrenching way she sobs. And now, the cutting edge of her screams, slicing through my heart like a knife.

I wouldn't say that Celia Monrovia deserves my brothers' torment, but for better or worse, they chose her... and she keeps choosing them. Over and over again, crawling into their beds, accepting their kisses, demanding their sacrifices—*oh, yes,* claiming Celia comes at a price that I don't think my brothers realize they're paying.

The three of them are lost, falling in love with a woman they have no business getting attached to.

The problem is that I might be falling with them.

I don't want to love anyone else. The three or four people who share the title of *loved one*—all of which I consider family, including Ezra Reinoff—have earned that title on account of saving my life and each other's.

Celia Monrovia has done neither of those things, yet she has poisoned my body to react to hers on a cellular level. When she screams, the hairs on my arms raise, and all I want to do is run towards her and catch her in my arms.

It's stupid, because there's a fucking net waiting to catch her, but I want it to be me. *I* want to be the one to fold her in my arms and kiss her tears away, and the urge to sweep her off of her dainty little feet and carry her to safety is so strong that I have to bar myself from interfering. I wrap my fists around a metal rung of a nearby ladder and grit my teeth as she bounces on her back into the net, choking on her fear as it consumes her.

My brother, ever the dramatist, jumps after her, leaping from thirty feet in the air. He's fucking crazy, too. Everything about this situation is insane. I never expected to walk through that door and find them together, nor did I expect to witness them having sex.

That's the *last* thing I ever, *ever* thought I'd find.

In truth, I wanted to catch her alone.

As always, I was too late.

Too late to win her heart before her ex-husband shattered it to pieces.

Too late to stop my brothers from claiming her for themselves.

Too late to protect her from their wicked intentions.

Because the moment she and Ruin tumble together in the middle of the net, I already know that she's theirs. She has been since the moment I met her in my bedroom; only then, I was too blind to see past my prejudice over who I thought she was to learn who my brothers had really fallen for.

Someone beautiful.

Someone damaged.

Someone that *can't* be mine.

I'm not a fool—I've seen the question in Rage's eyes when he catches me watching her. He wants to know how I'm feeling towards her. I haven't forgotten that punch to the face a few weeks ago—he won't let me hurt her, and for good reason.

I can be a real asshole.

But I catch myself in these moments with her—electrically charged, dangerous escalations that push my limits—and know that if given the chance, if my strength wanes, if she says anything to tip the scales between us—I'll fold.

Completely.

I take a breath as the sound of Celia's laughter, bright and loud and so full of life, fills the room. She's riding on the adrenaline high from the fall, and it's not me who's there to catch her—it's my brother, the biggest grin on his face as he rolls on top of her.

That is why I can't pursue Celia Monrovia.

Because I would be taking away from my brothers' joy.

Ruin reaches for a knife that is no longer attached to his hip. I whistle, pull a hidden switchblade from my boot, and flash it in the air over my head. Once he's caught on, I toss it towards him, and he catches it midair. Then he's carving through Celia's bindings, quickly cutting away the silk wrapped around her ankles and thighs to spread them apart.

I swallow hard as her laughter quickly turns into moans, breathless little sounds that go straight to my heart. *And my dick.* I squeeze my cock through the front of my dress pants, shuddering at the sound of Ruin's fingers inside of Celia's wet pussy.

She's *gushing*, and although I can't see it from this angle, I can hear it—the way she desires Ruin as much as she desires the others.

It's fucked up that I'm so goddamn jealous about it.

I scrub a hand down my face, but I can't turn around. I can't walk away. My feet move on their own, bringing me closer to them, the carnal need to watch her unravel clouding my judgement. This isn't consensual; she doesn't know that I'm here, but I can't look away.

I want to be in my brother's place.

Badly.

The net digs into her skin, no doubt marking her body more than the silk ever could. It's only a few feet over my head, dipping in the center where they lay, giving me a perfect view of her ass, her shoulders, the arch of her back—and of Ruin's face staring at me from between her thighs. His nostrils flare, but he doesn't say anything, still burying his fingers inside of her slick cunt. The sound is even more exquisite from up close, and her voice—tiny cries pierce the air with each breath she takes, making my cock swell even harder.

My earpiece clicks as either Rage or Ruin catch on. "What's that sound?" Rage asks. "Where are you?"

I stare up at Celia and Ruin, the flash of jealousy for my youngest brother quickly turning into possessiveness to keep this moment to ourselves. We don't need a bigger audience.

"Than? Did you find Celia?"

"I bet Ruin has her," Rebel sighs dreamily. "Man, I'd pay to see that."

"Are you with them?" Rage's voice is thick with tension. "Are you watching them?"

A bead of sweat drips down my back. Am I that easy to read?

"I know you saw us the other day," Rage continues, louder. "I know that you want her, too."

Rebel chuckles. "You're not exactly subtle."

What is this, roast Thanatos hour?

Ruin dips his head between Celia's thighs and lifts her leg higher for better access to her sweet center. *Fuck me.* He's going to be as ravenous as the rest of them now that he's had a taste.

Celia's voice pitches higher as she writhes over my head. "Ohmygod," she cries, "*Ruin!*"

"That was her!" Rebel cheers, laughing. "Fuck me, man. She must be *loud.*" A pause, then, "Tell us where you are. It's not fair for you to keep it a secret."

I swallow hard as Celia's cries grow in intensity, my dick damn near breaking my zipper open. I take steady breaths as she finally comes, her moan so loud that my balls draw up. Hissing through my teeth, I shove my hand down my pants and squeeze my dick at the base to keep from coming. I shouldn't have the discipline of a goddamn teenager, for fuck's sake.

With a growl, I calm the raging hormones trying to tear open the floodgates, successfully keeping my baser instincts at bay. Exhaling harshly, I clench my eyes shut and try to shake myself out of it.

My cock refuses to listen, standing at full attention and forcing me to consider the alternative: rubbing one out *really* quickly.

Celia takes deep breaths above me. "Don't ever do that again," she tells Ruin. I can picture her glaring at him, her cheeks all flushed with equal parts embarrassment and satisfaction. She wiggles to try to free her hands. "You *bit* me!"

Grunting, Ruin cuts through the knot at her wrists and loosens the ribbon. "You liked it."

I should move.

I should really, *really* move.

She's going to roll over and see me. She'll scream all over again at the depraved pervert jerking off to the sound of her voice, unable to stop himself as he strokes his fat cock to the fantasies in his head of her slamming down on his cock, her tits bouncing with each hard thrust of his hips, pistoning in and out at breakneck speed, ready to fucking explode—

The tiniest sound catches in my throat as I come all over my fist, like I've done a hundred times now, catching my load in my boxers like the fucking animal I am. My cock softens, but only marginally, my balls aching for another release.

Fuck me.

One isn't enough anymore. I need to bust *two* goddamn loads to empty my balls. I suck in a breath, still agonizing over my situation, when Celia suddenly rolls onto her side.

Our eyes meet through the net.

She gasps like *she's* the one caught masturbating to her brothers' lover, not the other way around. "Th-Thanatos!" she shrieks, stumbling as she tries and fails to move. The net dips with every push of her hands and knees, with Ruin sitting back, content to watch her struggle.

I tear my eyes away from the teeth marks on her tits to stare into the distance, then at the hand still buried in my pants. *Shit.* I quickly extricate my hand with a grimace and, without thinking, wipe the cum on my pant leg. "I, uh, came to find you."

Ruin suddenly snaps the sharp end of the knife against the holes in the net, quickly cutting themselves free. Celia shrieks as she falls straight into my arms, slamming against my chest. I catch her easily, ensuring that she isn't injured from damn near slamming into the floor. Her warmth is a welcome balm to the ache in my heart—if only for a moment. She jerks away from me as soon as her feet touch the ground. Unsteadily, she tumbles backward into Ruin's chest, my younger brother snaking his arms around her waist the moment their bodies collide.

"You—What are you doing here? Why were you—" Celia's eyes flick down to my crotch, her face burning deep crimson.

I quickly avert my eyes and clear my throat. "I came to make sure you were safe."

"Oh, *you came*, alright." Her eyes flash, and she pulls away from Ruin to jab my chest with her index finger. "Is that what you are, Thanatos? A stalker? Are you using me to get your rocks off?" Huffing, she crosses her arms to cover her chest. "Get a fucking girlfriend, then! Okay? Can you do that?"

I glare at her, the spitfire of a woman too wrapped up in her own problems to see mine. "I can't," I grind out, my teeth clenched so hard that my jaw hurts. "I fucking *can't*, Celia."

She doesn't back down, too amped up on adrenaline

or pride. "Why the hell not? You're—look at you!" She laughs, a loud burst of air in the cavernous space, and shakes her head. "You could have anyone here tonight, you know that? Any woman in that casino would *gladly* take you home. So, what are you doing here?" She unlatches her arms to shove my chest, no longer shy about being naked in front of me. "What are you *still* doing here, Thanatos? Because I'm—"

"Infuriating," I growl, cutting her off. My heartbeat pounds in my ears as weeks of frustration and anger rise up within me. "You are *insufferable*. Always whining about your goddamn business, walking around half-naked all the time, driving me *insane* with the sound of your fucking voice—"

She bristles. "Like you're a fucking peach!" She growls with her own frustration. Pitching her voice lower, she says, "I'm so big and macho, with my huge muscles and girthy cock; I like to throw girls around and pretend that I'm not grinding into their ass all morning, rocking the biggest hard on of my life! I can't wait to shove her against a wall and lecture her about *controlling her body*, when I can't even control my own!" Her eyes burn with a fire so hot that I feel it down to my toes, my entire body igniting from her flames. "You're such a self-righteous asshole!"

I grind my teeth, feeling my own fire burn inside my chest. "You're a fucking tease!"

"I'm not the one throwing myself at you!"

"Maybe not, but you don't tell me to stop, either! If you had told me 'no' even once—*just once, Celia*—then maybe I could get you out of my head. Just say no. Tell me that you don't want me. Go on, say it!"

She narrows her eyes and purses her lips. "Fine." Stepping up to me, she bumps my chest with her own, pressing her body against mine. "I don't want you," she growls, then she says it for a second time. "I *don't* want you." Her eyes flick down to my lips for a split second. "I don't."

"You don't," I repeat, pulled in by the heat of her body and the sweat on her skin. The smell of sex clings to her, and I breathe in deep, shuddering as raw *need* courses through me. I growl in frustration and tell myself *no*. Under no circumstances am I going to touch her right now. I'm going to walk away, because that's what's best for everyone. As soon as my business is done in this city, I'm walking away for good.

Celia Monrovia will never tempt me again.

"I don't," Celia mutters for the fourth time, her voice wavering at the end. "I *really* don't."

"Me either," I breathe, the tip of my nose brushing hers. "I really—"

"Really—"

Don't.

CHAPTER 19

RUIN

ALL CELIA NEEDS is a little courage, so I flatten my palms against her shoulders and...

Push.

She tips forward, caught off balance, and her mouth lands on Thanatos's, stunning them both into blessed silence. They were way too fucking loud. I exhale slowly, releasing some of the tension in my muscles as I continue holding her to the spot, rooting them together at the lips.

It doesn't bother me that they want to fuck each other. The only one of us it bothers—besides Rage, but he's got a jealousy problem—is the two of them, both of them too stubborn and prideful to get it over with. He likely thinks that he's stepping on our toes, and she might still hold animosity towards him for all of the hateful things he said to her.

I still remember every word, and I bet Celia does, too.

That's why they need to get all the poison out of their system so that they can start fresh. None of us will get any sleep at night if the two of them are at each other's throats, especially if we have a newborn baby screaming at all hours of the day. Hopefully, the baby will take after... whoever has the best temperament. Probably Thanatos, which is why I'm okay with him and Celia being together.

It makes sense.

Neither of them moves, so I slide up behind her and block her in with my hands on her hips and her back pressed to mine, the same way Rebel did for me when I first kissed Celia, or she first kissed me. I'm not too sure who moved first.

The same is happening here—both Thanatos and Celia colliding without words. Briefly, a flash of a memory of Celia and Rage being pushed together at the club comes to mind, but it fades the instant that Thanatos finally moves, his hands wrapping around Celia's fists. They're clenched so tightly that he has to pry them open, and then—and *only* then—do either of them remember to breathe. Her eyes flutter open to find that his are shut, her lips parting as he deepens the kiss, pouring his weight onto her, and then onto me. I take a step back and she stumbles, but Thanatos is quick to catch her, dragging her back to his body and grabbing her hip to steady her.

They stare at each other with half-lidded gazes, drunk on the adrenaline flowing through their veins, standing at a crossroads.

Will they continue tugging this thread loose, or will they choose to tie themselves into knots over the clear attraction between them?

Clicking on my earpiece, I sigh. "We're in the acrobat room. Employee entrance."

"Fucking *finally*," Rebel whines, making me flinch. My head throbs, and I quickly remove the ear bud and slip it into my pocket. That's enough stimulation for one night, thank you. I reach into my back pocket and pull out a blunt, quickly lighting it and taking a deep pull. The smoke flows past my lips in a lazy haze as I watch Celia and Than.

They still haven't moved.

"Let me go," she whispers, fisting the front of his shirt and doing absolutely nothing about how he's holding her.

"I can't," Than breathes, his eyebrows pinching together. "I can't do that, Princess."

She huffs, a single punch of air passing her lips. "Why not?"

His answer is immediate. "I don't want to."

Biting her bottom lip, she draws his eye to her mouth. "We can't do this."

"We can't."

"We *can't.*"

With a frustrated growl, Thanatos cups her cheek and tilts her head back. "We fucking *can.*" His lips crash into hers, earning a heady moan from our girl. He plucks her lips between his and slides his fingers into her hair, snagging on the knots. She moans again, wrapping her hand around the base of his neck and pulling him in, deepening their connection.

I almost feel like an intruder, but I *was* here first.

Slipping my hands into my front pockets while pinching the blunt between my teeth, I watch the two of them fight for dominance. She bites his lip, and he bites back, their breaths short and quick as if they're worried the moment will be over in the blink of an eye.

Nothing more than a wet dream.

Thanatos has dreamt of this—I can see it in the way he touches her, running his hands through her hair and across her cheeks, sighing into her mouth like a man who has waited for this his entire life.

Celia, on the other hand, is trembling from head to foot, clinging to his neck and shoulders like a lifeline. She touches the raised scar on his cheek, then the one cutting through his lip, a long-forgotten knife having made its mark.

As I slip Than's switchblade into my boot and pick up my hunting knife from the floor, the door to the casino swings open. Rage and Rebel push through one after the other, with Rebel grinning like a cat while Rage broods like a bull. They approach quickly, not caring for stealth. As the door snaps shut, Thanatos and Celia jerk back, the two of them startled apart. Celia's face is flushed a pretty pink, while Thanatos's ears burn bright red.

Hm. Maybe they weren't ready, after all.

She wraps her arm around mine and grabs my hand,

standing boldly on display. I remove the blunt from my teeth and grab her chin, pulling her face up to mine to exhale into her mouth. Her pretty eyes widen, but she inhales like a good girl, coughing after a moment. I press my nose to her temple and smile, enjoying the smell of me on her skin. Smoking with her is going to be *fun.*

"Well, well, well," Rebel muses cheekily as he comes to a stop in front of us, grinning from ear to ear. "What do we have here? Having fun, baby?" He winks as he looks between the three of us, me with Celia to the left, while Thanatos stands alone to the right. "If I'd known we were having a party, I would have brought champagne."

"This isn't funny," Rage snaps, glaring at everyone. "You can't turn off your comms. You can't ignore—" He growls, gnashing his teeth and pacing in a tight line between us and Rebel. After taking a deep breath and pinching the bridge of his nose, he finally looks up at Celia. "Are you hurt?" His eyes scan her body, his lips twitching at all of the marks on her skin.

My smile spreads, and I chuckle into Celia's hair.

She's mine now, too, Rage. Body *and* soul.

My older brother might have gotten there first, but my touch will linger the longest. I brush my knuckles over the bruises on her right breast, enjoying the sharp intake of her breath as I graze her nipple.

"I'm fine, Rage. I told you that I was okay."

"You promised," he murmurs, flicking his gaze to mine. "Is she okay, Ruin?"

"Crystal," I sigh, taking another pull from my blunt. I lift an eyebrow at Celia, and she tilts her chin up, allowing me to exhale into her mouth again. Electricity zings down my spine as the transfer turns into a kiss, her lips soft and warm and sweet on mine.

This could get very addicting, *very* quickly.

"That doesn't even make sense," Rebel chuckles, "but whatever. She's fine, Rage, can't you see?" He waves his hand, gesturing towards Celia. "She's got that glow."

I frown, pulling away from Celia to stare at my brother. "What glow?"

If he takes her soul from me—

"You know, *the glow.* That well-fucked look. Your hair's a mess, baby." Rebel snickers as he steps up to us and runs his fingers through Celia's long, soft waves, pulling them over her shoulders so that the ends kiss the top of her breasts. Admiring her appearance, he smirks, then leans in to steal a kiss from her pouty lips. "Mmm. Give me a hit, Ruin." He tilts his head to the side for me to place the blunt between his lips, then takes a deep breath, the tip of the roll burning bright orange. Once he's gotten enough, he cups Celia's face in both hands and seals their lips together, smiling as they share the smoke.

Their transfer also turns into a kiss, Rebel quickly sliding his tongue between her lips and moaning.

"None of you should be getting high," Thanatos sighs, running a hand through his hair. His neck is still flushed, and despite his chastisement, he's staring at Celia like he wants another taste. He unbuttons his vest and shucks it off, leaving it on the floor. Sweat makes his dress shirt cling to his skin, the material thin enough that we can see the tattoos across his chest. "Tonight isn't about having fun, it's about—"

"Killing our dad," Rage interrupts, scowling at him. "That's rich, coming from the man who just had his tongue down my wife's throat."

Rebel moans again, kissing Celia harder and grabbing her ass to haul her body against his.

"You're not married," Thanatos counters, his eyes narrowing. "I'd never take her from you, you know that."

"But you'll fuck her when my back is turned, is that it?"

Sighing, Rebel pulls away from Celia's lips to rest his forehead against hers. "Guys, c'mon, do you really want to argue while she's still naked? She's even—" A shudder racks his body as he slides his fingers between her thighs —"you *have* to see feel this. Baby, lie down for me. That's it. Good girl." As he helps her onto her back, all four of us crowd around. "Spread your legs, beautiful. Don't be shy."

Blushing furiously, Celia obeys, covering her face with her forearm. "I can't *believe* we're doing this."

"Believe it, baby. Now look, boys. You see that?" He licks his lips. "That's *our* pussy. This is *our* girl. She wants us all to share. Isn't that right, Celia?"

There's a beat of silence before she whispers a quiet *yes.*

"You've gotta say it louder or they won't believe it."

"Yes!"

I stare at Celia's glistening pussy, my cum coating her lips and clit.

Yeah, that's mine, too.

I glance at each of my brothers and notice that not only are they all staring at her wet pussy, but all three of them are suddenly rock hard, their dicks tenting their pants. I take another hit of my blunt, my own cock twitching back to life. "We can't all fuck her at once."

Rebel smirks. "Can't we?"

"Rebel!" Celia throws her arm down to glare at him. "You most certainly *can not!*" She closes her thighs and pushes up onto her elbows. Once she sees how hard everyone is, she can't stop staring at our crotches. "Listen, I know this is a little unorthodox—"

One of my brothers snorts out loud.

She glares at the culprit. "—but I really do want..." She bites her lip. "All of you. Maybe we can take turns."

Rage falls to his knees and grabs both of hers, slowly prying them open. "No."

No?

I tilt my head to the side as he caresses her creamy thighs. Rage always thinks that he's in charge, but if Celia is the one we all want... wouldn't that make her the boss?

What's the saying—*wearing the pants*?

I rub my eyes and pass the blunt to Rebel. He would understand it, I think, but from where I'm standing, Celia is the only one of us naked right now. She has no pants.

At the moment.

Rage cups Celia's pussy and pushes his fingers inside, then he gathers what cum remains around her lips and pushes *that* inside, too. She whimpers, her face burning and chest heaving. "Wh-what are you doing?"

He exhales slowly, tearing his eyes away from her cunt to study her face. "*We* are going to get you pregnant, mama. If that means that Thanatos is a part of this... if you *really* want him, too..." Gently, he removes his fingers and holds them up to her lips. "Who am I to say no?" He pushes his fingers inside of her mouth, coating her tongue in my cum and hers. "Lick me clean, love. Good." He swallows at the same time she does, then pulls his hand back and grabs her thigh. "I'm not thrilled about sharing you with another man. I'm not going to lie about that." With his other hand, he undoes his belt, freeing his cock and stroking it hard, a muscle in his jaw jumping. "But I promised that I would do anything to give you the life you want, so I will." His breathing grows harsh. "Are you ready for it, mama?" Tipping his head back, he groans. "Because I'm ready."

She glances up at me, then at the procession of men standing—and kneeling—before her. Biting her lip, she sits up and crawls on her knees to Rage, straddling his thick thighs before slowly, *very slowly*, lowering her pussy over his cock. He groans deeply as he bottoms out, grabbing the back of her head and slamming her lips over his. She cries out, the sound lost to Rage's growls as he punches his hips up to meet hers.

I know that her pussy is sore. Her body, too, if the rope burns criss-crossing her skin mean anything. I lick

my lips, ignoring the swell of my cock to enjoy the view
for what it is.

A perfect moment.

The beginning of the end.

Till death do us part, krosotka.

CHAPTER 20

CELIA

MY BODY ACHES in ways that I never thought possible, and in *places* that I never knew existed. Not only are my upper arms sore right where they meet my armpit, but my *ass* is sore, my skin stinging from what little time Ruin and I spent hanging in the net.

I guess being naked can cause more problems than I thought.

But *this*—the hot pulse of Rage's thick cock filling me up with his cum—this isn't a problem.

It's a miracle.

I'm amazed that we ever made it this far without him tying me down and forcing himself into my body to knock me up in a self-proclaimed act of love. He cradles the back of my head and stares into my eyes, breathing hard as he lays me down on the mat and lifts my legs into the air to tilt my hips back, ensuring that as little of his seed escapes as possible. His brothers watch, all three of them entranced by the sight of my swollen, cock-abused pussy.

It's Thanatos's intense stare that I find the most embarrassing, so I avoid his eyes and stare up at the ceiling instead. All things considered, this position is pretty comfortable, and I find myself relaxing as Rage rubs the back of my thighs, digging his palms in to massage my sore muscles. Someone else joins him and rubs the swell of my left calf, and then another takes my right. I bite my lip to keep from moaning at the sweet relief flooding my system—moaning or *crying*.

Tears fill my eyes, and I hold my breath to keep them from spilling over. None of this feels real, especially the part about having three men kneel to caress my aching muscles, but I'm starting to believe that a natural sense of awe at our situation is a good thing. "Thank you," I murmur, chancing a glance at my men.

All three of them have the softest looks on their faces, their lips curving into smiles as individual as their personalities. Rebel's hooks the most at one end, skewing towards a smirk, while Rage's pride is on full display in the broad stretch of his lips. Ruin, however, has the smallest smile of them all, a quiet upturn of his lips that softens the rest of his face, his smile hiding how depraved he truly is.

Thanatos is the only one of them still standing, looking out of place with his arms crossed and head turned to the side, like he shouldn't be here at all. The reddening blush trailing down his neck gives him away, though. I know that if I weren't looking at him, he would be staring directly at me.

I hold out my hand and gesture for him to come closer. He watches me out of the corner of his eye for a long moment, his jaw clenching as he considers his options. Accept the naked woman's offer, or…

Is there really a choice?

Slowly, he shuffles over to join us. He looks at his brothers as though expecting their protest, then drops to his knees by my side, taking my hand in his. He brushes the pads of my fingers with his calloused fingertips and stares at the junction of our hands. "How long do we wait for… this?" His blush deepens, blooming across his cheeks.

"I don't know about you guys, but I'm *starving.*" With a laugh, I pull my legs free. "Please take me to get something to eat. Oh, and to a bathroom. First. Bathroom *first.* Or I'll smell like a—" My nose crinkles as I think of all the things I could say. The one that sticks out the most, however, echoes through my mind in Thanatos's gravelly baritone.

She smells like a whore.

Our eyes suddenly meet, like he's remembering the exact same moment. "Like a lover," he says firmly, trying to rewrite our past. "It's a good… smell on you."

Rebel snorts, angling his face to grin at his eldest brother. "It's a good look on her, too. You're fucking ravishing, baby. I can't wait to bury my dick inside of you."

I bite my lip as my pussy throbs, aching and full.

There's no way I can take another dick right now, or even tomorrow. Or the *next* day. "I think I need a break," I say honestly, allowing Thanatos and Rage to pull me to my feet. "I won't be much of a lover if my pussy breaks."

"Impossible," Rebel dismisses quickly, pressing a quick kiss to my cheek. "We haven't even put two cocks in there yet. *Then* we'll worry about breaking your pussy in, baby."

Two... cocks?

"In one hole?" I grab Rebel's arm as my jaw drops. "There's no way!" Glancing at the others, I feel my face burn like I've been lit on fire. None of them seem remotely surprised. "No way, I can't fit *two* of you in there! That's insane!"

"Or *really* hot," Rebel muses, smirking like he's been planning this all along. "If you've already got a load inside of you, it's extra lubrication. Makes the job easier."

He *has* been thinking about this!

"Ohmygod," I moan, covering my face with my hands. "I'm dating a nymphomaniac."

"Dating?" Rage rumbles, glaring daggers at Rebel. "You're *marrying* me, mama, and I'm not a fucking nympho."

"Not yet," Rebel chuckles. "Just wait until we both get inside of her at once, man. You'll change your mind."

"We are *not* talking about this!" I smack Rebel's chest as he grins, then I catch Rage staring at me intently, the gears clearly turning in his head. "I can't believe you two! It's my body. I get to choose what or who or—" I swallow hard. "Or how many go in there!"

Ruin shoulders Rebel out of the way and offers me his blunt, holding it up to my lips. I know that I shouldn't—we're supposed to be luring out a serial killer, after all—but I might need something for my aching body... I take the tiniest puff imaginable and can't hold in my cough, but Ruin quickly takes a drag and grabs my chin, pulling my lips to his and exhaling into my mouth.

The smoke is easier to take when one of them gives it to me, especially when it turns into a full-blown kiss. Ruin slides his lips over mine with a satisfied hum that sends tingles down my spine, making me shiver.

"She's cold," Than murmurs somewhere in the distance. The next thing I know, he and Rage are trying to sort out which side of my dress is the top versus the bottom, while Rebel pulls a simple black strip of lace from his back pocket.

"I think you've earned these," he muses, kneeling to help me into my panties. He carefully slips them past my feet and up my thighs, gently kissing my stomach on his way back up my body. His brothers finally figure out how a beaded dress works, and I quickly put my clothes back on, heels included. Ruin buttons up his shirt, but Thanatos leaves his vest off, crumpling it into a ball and tossing it into an empty trash can.

Rage looks like he wants to say something about it, but he swallows his thought and jerks his head toward the door. "C'mon, let's get you cleaned up, and then we'll find you something to eat." He wraps my arm around his and takes my hand firmly in his. Brushing his lips over my ear, he rumbles, "it's my turn, now, *krosotka*, but tonight is *your* night. We're going to celebrate."

I turn my head until our eyes meet, my heart stuttering at how drop-dead gorgeous he is. High cheekbones, intense, charcoal eyes, firm grip on my hand. Out of all of the brothers, he's the only one wearing a coat and tie, with a hint of a five o'clock shadow brushing across his jaw. He looks the most like a gentleman out of the bunch, but I know better. He'll touch me in front of a room full of people if it means proving that I'm his. But maybe we've grown enough over the past few weeks that he can believe it without provocation.

Maybe this time, I can be the one to prove to him that I'm his.

Squeezing his hand, I press my lips to his in a slow, sensual kiss that I hope he understands. I close my eyes and lean into his chest, sighing against his lips. "Thank you," I murmur, enjoying the way he doesn't take any more from the moment, doesn't demand that the kiss be longer or harder or more passionate.

Rage brushes his knuckles against my jaw as he stares into my eyes. "There's never a need to thank me." He exhales, slowly working up the courage to say more. "I could make up every single thing I've ever done to hurt you, and it still wouldn't be enough." His eyes slide closed. "I want to *earn* you, Celia... if you'll let me."

I never thought I would see such a proud, dominant man bending for anyone, let alone me. The woman he's been after ever since the day we met. The one he collared and locked inside of a cage. The one he beat another man bloody for touching. The one he vowed to make fall in love with him.

The longer he looks at me like I'm the one thing he can't live without, the closer I am to believing that it's true.

I might fall in love with Rage...

Tonight.

Chapter 21

Celia

The venue for the gala is split into sections: the faux casino in the main room with multiple cash bars dispersed throughout, the adjacent ballrooms hosting various shows and silent auctions, and an outdoor dining experience in the oncoming winter.

Someone didn't consult the women before deciding to host a three course meal outside. Despite the standing heat lamps surrounding the perimeter, the winter bite in the air is harsh enough to make me shiver. I wrap my faux fur shawl tighter around me, appreciating its warmth but needing more as a chill sweeps across my legs.

Rage and I weave through the round dining tables for our name cards until he finds our entire party at a table for eight. I check each name, my curiosity at an all-time high. He lifts an eyebrow as I circle the table. "You're right here." Grabbing the back of my assigned seat, he pulls it away from the table to make room for me to sit.

"What about yours?"

He nods to the space beside mine. "I'm next to you."

I glance at the remaining cards but barely see the names, my curiosity over Rage's card getting the better of me. Hopping around the table in excitement, I bounce on the balls of my feet as I check our place settings. The name on my card is as expected, Celia Monrovia, but Rage's...

"Nikolai Cheknekov?" I take in his appearance from top to bottom, admiring how well his name fits. "Is that real or fake?"

Patting the top of my chair, he smirks. "Wouldn't you like to know?"

Rolling my eyes with a smile, I take my seat and allow him to push me in. "Yes, actually, I would." I lean to each side to check the surrounding names, all ending in Cheknekov.

Emil.

Yuri.

Thanatos.

"Why is Thanatos the only one using his real name? Does that mean that yours—" I squeal in excitement. "Can I call you Nikolai?"

Rage brings the back of my hand to his lips and kisses my knuckles, chuckling under his breath. "Only in bed, *krosotka*."

I gasp. "Deal." I contain my eagerness while the server fills our wine glasses with a charming red, but the moment he's gone, I read the other cards again and mutter the names under my breath, getting a feel for each one. "So which one is Emil and which is Yuri?"

"You'll have to ask them."

My earpiece clicks on, Rebel's voice suddenly in my head. "No way, you *cannot* call me anything other than Rebel. Not even in bed!"

"Are you sure?" I sit back in my chair and sip my wine. "I bet your name sounds really good on my lips. *Especially* if I'm moaning." Flicking my eyes to Rage, I let out a breathy whimper. "*Nikolai,*" I tease, "harder, please! *Ah!* I'm gonna—I'm gonna—"

The table beside ours pauses their conversation to peek over at us, and I die of laughter. Setting down my glass, I wipe my mouth with my cloth napkin and clear my throat, regaining my composure. "See? Imagine that, but with the name Emil or Yuri on my lips—"

"Celia," Rage rumbles, his burning hand dropping to my thigh. "I said that you could use it while *in bed*, not at the dinner table." His eyes smolder like embers as he squeezes just above my knee. "Keep teasing me, and I'll put you on your knees beneath it."

My eyes widen as my heart skips a beat. "You wouldn't."

Rage's smile sharpens, turning wolfish. "Say my name again and find out."

We're still staring at each other when Rebel suddenly appears, slipping in front of the place setting beside mine, the one labeled for *Emil.* He drapes his arm over the back of his chair and runs his other hand through his hair, mussing it up even more than it already was. "Celia, baby, you can't go around moaning like that, or we'll all go crazy." Licking a stripe across his top row of teeth, he smiles just as predatorily as Rage. "I'll fuck you on this table in front of the whole staff."

Nerves bubble up like champagne inside my stomach as I look between the two of them. I doubt they're serious... right? With a tight smile, I down the rest of my wine before grabbing Rage's untouched glass. "Please don't."

One blow job in front of an entire club was enough for me.

Rage's entire demeanor changes in an instant. "Then we won't." He grabs Rebel's shoulder and squeezes, making the other man wince. "Leave, brother."

Rebel whines loudly. "Man, I'm hungry, too! Let me eat!"

"Go find something else."

"But this is catered! I picked the steak!"

"You can take it to-go when we leave."

A couple approaches our table, the woman smiling at us while her partner pulls out her seat. I give her a quick smile before turning back to my men, but then an icy shiver rolls down my spine as a flare of recognition goes off in my brain. I flinch as she says my name, her voice eerily familiar.

"Is that you, Celia? We haven't seen you since the—" Charlotte's smile pinches as she looks over her shoulder at Caleb "Teddy" Kissinger, the man stunned into awkward silence as he stares directly at me.

My ex-husband Ted.

"Since the divorce," I finish for her, forcing my smile to stick. "How funny to bump into you here."

It's not funny at all.

"Darling," I say to Rage, grabbing his lapel. "Why don't we come back later? I'm not that hungry after all." Nausea broils in my gut, turning my mood sour. I haven't seen Ted in person in years, keeping to internet stalking him and his new wife Charlotte. She arches her back and holds out her hand for his to get his attention, and that's when I see it.

The baby bump.

"You're expecting," I cry, somehow unable to shut up. "Oh, how wonderful. You must be overjoyed."

Both Rebel and Rage share a look before turning to the couple seated across from us. Ruin grunts in my ear and then murmurs something, but I'm too blinded by hurt so deep to understand what he's saying.

Ted is having a baby.

While I'm *still* childless.

Charlotte smiles politely. "Thank you. This will be our second. We're hoping for a girl this time."

Rebel's fingers immediately twine in mine on the table, in direct view of Ted and Charlotte, while Rage's hand travels beneath the slit in my skirt to stroke my bare skin. "You need to eat," Rage says gently. "Why don't you introduce us to your friends?"

I close my eyes and nod once. I can do this. It's not that hard to pretend that my heart isn't breaking all over again. I've done it a thousand times; I'm sure I can do it again. "Nikolai," I say, opting to use Rage's real name.

"Emil," I continue, also using Rebel's. As easy as it is to lie to strangers about a name, the last thing I want to do now is claim that these men—Rage or Nikolai, Rebel or Emil—are anything *but* mine.

It doesn't matter what we call each other as long as we stay together.

"This is Ted and Charlotte. My ex-husband and his new wife." I loop my fingers around Rage's tie, unclipping it from his shirt. "These are my boyfriends," I say to the other couple, keeping my smile as bright as possible. "They own a night club in the city."

Ted sits beside his wife, his eyes pinging between the three of us. "That's..." He doesn't finish his sentence, choosing to swallow instead. Reaching for his water glass, he drinks half in one go. "Huh."

"Huh?" Rebel's smile ripples before it falls. "What does that mean?"

"Let it go, Emil," Rage says quickly. "Teddy is simply awestruck that his ex-wife is doing so well. We take good care of her." Grabbing my thigh, he makes me jump, my knees knocking into the underside of the table. "*And* she's killing it with her fashion line. Isn't that one of your designs, Celia?" He nods towards Charlotte's cream-colored sweater dress. "I think I recognize it from last winter's collection."

My blood pressure rises as I realize that I *have* to look at her again. Carefully, I turn my head to check Charlotte's dress and try not to stare at her baby bump.

Rage is completely correct; that's one of my most popular dresses from a year ago.

Of course, he also knows that he's correct. I catch him staring at me with all the pride in the world, his thumb stroking gentle arcs into my skin beneath the table. "You have good tastes," I say finally, feeling a little better. Seeing one of my designs out in the wild—and not a custom one for this evening—is always a treat. "It's a beautiful color for your complexion."

"Thank you!" As the server brings a wooden serving board of freshly baked bread to our table, she asks for pats of real butter rather than the oil and balsamic vinegar already set out. Eying the bread, she knocks the back of her hand against Ted's chest. "Would you slice the bread for the table?"

"Gladly," Rebel cuts in, tugging the board to our side of the table. He grabs the bread knife and holds it up for us all to admire. Flames from the fire pit in the center of the dining area flicker in the blade's mirrored edge. "Funny thing about knives," he says slowly, touching the sharp, serrated tips. "They sure know how to stab you in the back. Especially when you're distracted."

"Especially," Rage repeats, watching as Rebel begins slicing the loaf into equal-sized pieces. He only cuts four, then slides them onto four identical plates and sets them in front of everyone... except for Ted. Charlotte's butter arrives, and she carefully unwraps a rectangle, her hands shaking as she swipes her butter knife across the side. After she covers her slice of bread, she gently pushes the bowl to our side of the table, her smile as soft as her eyes.

Kind eyes for a gentle woman.

She doesn't deserve this testosterone-fueled, dick-measuring contest.

"Why don't you boys take Ted to the bar for a drink," I suggest, squeezing both Rage and Rebel's hands. "And send for another loaf of bread for the table."

Rebel's face falls. "What? Why would we—"

"Of course," Rage interjects, meeting my eyes. "Whatever you need."

Relief washes over me. "Thank you." I squeeze his hand a second time. "I need more bread and butter."

And Charlotte doesn't need to watch my men tear Ted apart with their eyes.

"You boys have fun."

Ted visibly pales. Although he isn't part of the bratva, after our divorce, I heard a rumor that my brother Mikhail paid him a visit. A very long, very painful visit. There really isn't any need for Rage or Rebel to do anything to him, especially now that he and Charlotte are expecting a baby, but...

It won't kill him to sweat a little.

As Rebel slides his chair back to stand, I take the bread knife from his hands. "Play nice," I tell him, pursing my lips. "You're going to be a dad soon. Maybe you can learn something from him."

Both Rebel and Thanatos chuff at the same time, one of them directly in front of me and one through the speaker in my ear. I catch the eldest Cheknekov brother watching from the other side of the dining area, his arms crossed as he stands like a bouncer in front of the red velvet ropes separating the tables from the dark back lawn. Beyond the lush expanse of the out-of-season green grass lies a patch of trees, and beyond that, the mountain that separates the city from the rest of the state.

Charlotte catches me staring at our shadowed backdrop and sighs. "Yeah, it's pretty ominous, sitting here after all the bodies they found on the mountainside." She shakes her head, then takes a bite of bread and moans. "You have to try this, Celia. It's sooo fresh!"

I'm still stuck on the first thing she said. "What bodies?"

She finishes her slice and grabs a second from Rebel's plate. "You haven't heard? They found an open pit with at least a dozen people thrown inside. All dead. All women. The police think that they were tourists staying in the cabins up near the lake. So sad." Taking another bite of bread, she sighs as she chews. "It's almost Christmas, and all of those families will be missing their loved ones." Her eyes well with tears, and she hastily brushes them away. "Sorry, it's the hormones!"

A pang of jealousy hits my heart like a hammer. "It's okay."

"Is it, though?" A strand of blonde hair falls from her updo. "So many people have died. And then your boutique!" Her eyes widen as she jumps from topic to topic. "I saw the pictures! It's a miracle that no one was there when it burned down."

Yeah, definitely a miracle.

I pull off a small piece of the soft middle part of my bread and chew it slowly, wondering where Ruin is right now. Did he disappear into the shadows again, or is he actively looking for his dad in the crowd? I know that we got distracted earlier, but I can't find it in my heart to regret it, despite the risks.

More people could be in danger right now... yet here I am, breaking bread with the woman who stole my ex-husband from me.

"When did they find the bodies on the mountain?" Lifting my eyes, I stare at the jagged outline of dark rock towering in the distance over the tree line. The snow caps have grown with the oncoming winter, making it a popular skiing destination. How could an entire population of people miss a mass grave?

"Oh, I don't know. Ted's the one who told me. Ted!" Charlotte calls out for her husband, swiveling in her chair to look for him. "Now where did he go..." The closest bar to us is missing two tall, violent men and their latest target.

Shit. I feel a little bad about that. "Emil probably kidnapped him to play poker. He's been on a winning streak. Says that he wants to take money from everyone's pockets." I sip my wine and listen for my men in our comms unit, but they've gone silent. I check for Thanatos near the lawn, and he's still there, saying something to the others that I can't hear.

Chuckling, Charlotte relaxes. "Ted's got a shit hand at poker. Emil's going to clean him out."

Tilting my head to the side, I study Charlotte, admiring her pregnancy glow. "Are you happy, Charlotte? Does Ted... is he good to you?" I can't fathom that the man who used to ignore me for days after seeing a negative pregnancy test would learn to be a good husband, not even to Charlotte. She seems really nice, and Ted slowly lost his kindness throughout our marriage.

I wonder if I put too much pressure on him when we were married. To be perfect. Maintain appearances. Keep up with my baby fever. Although none of that condones Ted's actions, they may have contributed towards his affair, and Charlotte, despite her gentle appearance, was a part of that.

She places her hands in her lap. "Our marriage isn't perfect, but that's life, isn't it? I'm happy because we try our best every day, and I can't ask for more than that. He's a good father." Inclining her head towards me, she smiles. "And I know that you'll make a wonderful mother, Celia. I've always thought that, even before Ted and I started dating. I know that you both wanted children. But sometimes... we need to be with the right people first." Gently holding her round belly, she smiles. "I'm with my person. Are you with yours?"

I hadn't expected for this conversation to become emotional. I look over Charlotte's shoulder at Thanatos, feeling something stir inside my heart. He's infuriating. Insufferable. Drives me insane—just like the rest of them.

Our damaged, loyal, crazy little family.

When Thanatos finally looks back over at me, I let the warm, fluttery feeling expand until I'm smiling at him. "Yeah, I am with my people."

All four of them.

CHAPTER 22

RUIN

THERE'S something moving in the woods.

While my brothers fight over the best kind of knife to stab Ted with—a carving knife, obviously—I walk across the back lawn to get a better look at the forest, ignoring the mountain for the trees. They sway in a cold breeze, rustling their long, spindly branches. The moon is waning, which means that the nights have been getting darker and colder with each one that passes. The closer we get to the winter solstice, the longer those nights become.

It's easier to hide bodies in the winter. Fewer people exploring the outdoors means that there are less chances for people to catch you in the act of burning or burying a body. Yet my father has managed to expose every single kill he's made, because he's done a terrible job hiding them.

Or, more likely, he isn't trying to keep them a secret.

Whoever dug a mass grave on the mountainside is either stupid... or hoping that someone notices.

Someone like me.

I hadn't heard the news about the bodies; with our focus being within city lines, anything that our police scanners picked up that was past the line, we ignored. Or at least, I did. Thanatos has no reason to have missed that news, so he either thought it wasn't important for us to know, or...

He was distracted.

I can hear their banter in my ear, even from this distance. Rage and Rebel are interrogating Ted to scare the shit out of him, while Thanatos keeps watch of our girl. That's three men distracted, their focus for the evening being on making sure that Celia is both safe and having a good time.

Although my brothers could argue that I've *also* been distracted, I wasn't spending my time counting cards at the blackjack table or staring at Celia's ass from across the casino—I was actually working, keeping tabs on everyone who walked through the front doors. Only once the doors closed and no more guests were being admitted did I let my attention wander.

A shiver rolls down my spine, less from the cold and more from the memory of Celia's skin bruising beautifully beneath my teeth. I thought that my knife was going to be my favorite tool to touch her with, but I was quickly proven wrong by the sounds she made as I sunk my teeth into her flesh. I lick the roof of my mouth, imagining the taste of her blood on my tongue, and shiver again.

I can't wait for another taste.

But whatever is moving through the woods towards the bright lights of the gala is unhurried, taking its sweet time to get anywhere. It sways back and forth, unsteady on its feet or paws, as pale as the fading moon overhead. Only when it passes the tree line do I know what I'm looking at, and I quickly look around to check for event security. Of course, they're focused on keeping the guests safe and secure *inside*, thinking that their cameras and motion detectors will keep them safe from rodents and fleas hopping across their lawns.

No one in their right mind would walk down the side of a mountain.

That's how I know that the woman stumbling through the underbrush isn't in her right mind—especially when I realize that not only is she barefoot, but she's completely naked.

I pat my pockets, looking for my phone. Once I realize that I left it in Rage's car, I frown and tap my earpiece with my fingertip. "Hey. Turn off her comms."

Thanatos is the one who responds. "Why? What have you found?"

"Turn them off," I repeat, stepping over an anthill on my way toward the naked woman. "Then get the doctor." It was Than's idea to have a medical team on standby in case any of us were injured tonight, and I'm sure he's thrilled for them for actually be needed.

It doesn't look like our father is going to show.

As I jog toward the trees, I keep an eye out for more people, not nearly satisfied enough when the shadows don't move. Even the crickets are hiding, keeping their distance from whoever this woman is—or whoever is coming after her.

Predators don't let their prey loose without a reason. If she isn't dead yet, she will be as soon as she's accomplished her purpose.

I need to find out what that is.

"Hey," I call out, scrubbing at the scars on my cheek. I don't have time to be self-conscious about them, but in the end, it doesn't matter. The woman's eyes are glossy and unfocused, her feet moving without rhyme or reason. She steps on rocks, snaps branches beneath her feet, stumbles into the uncut grass, and keeps moving forward despite the cuts and bruises all over her body. I spot burn scars on her arms, recently made, which make my own itch. "Hey," I try again, clapping my hands. "Wake up."

There's at least a half mile between the gala and the forest, and I carry the woman the rest of the way back, careful to check that she's still breathing for the entire trip. She doesn't blink and doesn't speak, her lips hinging open and back shut every few seconds, her eyelids fluttering without closing.

Thanatos meets me at the side of the venue, a scowl on his face as he checks his phone. Guests are required to check theirs at the door, yet he managed to keep it. Sensing my question, he shakes his head. "Doesn't matter. Where did you find her?" Stepping forward, he brushes the raven hair from her eyes and curses, ushering me through an unguarded door. "Sara, hey, hold on. We've got a doctor. Stay with us."

"This is Sara?"

He clenches his jaw. "Yeah, that's her."

What was she doing outside?

We check for security before darting ahead toward our team's setup on the far end of the lot, the two of us keeping to the shadows beside the building to avoid detection. A few cameras are mounted overhead, so we'll have to remember to scrub the evidence and bribe whoever watches the feed.

"Do you think it was him?" I ask, ignoring the dread swirling in my gut. If it wasn't our father, then there's another cruel bastard kidnapping and murdering people in our area. Part of keeping bratva activities under the radar is monitoring your territory and its occupants; something as big as this going unchecked spells bad news for the Baranovas. "She's really pale."

Thanatos glances over his shoulder at her, his scowl deepening. "Yeah, she is. Check for track marks."

I angle our bodies so that the light spilling from a nearby balcony falls across the girl in my arms, and we work together to check her for marks, finding over a dozen along her arms and between her fingers.

Scrubbing a hand through his salt and pepper hair, my elder brother frowns as he stares at Sara's limp body. "Sakovia didn't answer his phone, but Serena says they're ready at the van. C'mon. We don't have much time."

My attention wavers as I stare at Sara. She looks close

to a corpse with sunken eyes and dry, cracked lips. My concern doesn't linger with the girl, however, quickly switching targets as Celia's bright smile flashes in my mind. "How is Celia? Did she hear anything?" If she sees Sara like this, I'm not sure how she'll react. Relieved that we found her? Horrified at the state she's in? Or angry and ready for blood? It's hard to know, but my body burns at the prospect of seeing it hit her all at once. Which one will dominate—the desire for revenge or the anguish from the loss of life?

We both fall silent as we cross the final stretch of lawn to our destination. I listen to what our brothers and Celia are up to now. Her microphone has been off since Thanatos disconnected her earpiece from his cell phone, but Rage and Rebel's voices are clear. They're trying to convince her to watch one of the shows. I can hear her asking for Thanatos in the background.

It must be killing him to ignore her.

"He was standing right there, and then all of a sudden, he looked at me and… ran off."

"Maybe he had to pee *really* badly."

Thanatos visibly deflates at Rebel's suggestion.

"Stop lying to me. I know that something is wrong."

"I'm not lying," Rebel says unconvincingly, his voice lilting at the end. He never was a good liar.

She turns her ire onto Rage. "My earbud isn't working. What did you do?"

"I didn't do anything." At least Rage can be honest about that. "Eat your salmon."

"Tell me where Thanatos and Ruin are."

The corners of my mouth curve into a smile. Hearing my name on Celia's lips is quickly going to become a favorite of mine.

Once we reach the van, Than knocks loudly on the side window. "Open up."

Using a cargo van as a mobile trauma station was Than's idea, but Ezra was the one who approved the setup. It's been gutted from top to bottom, save the two seats in the front, in order to transform into a discreet ambulance, complete with a stretcher, a dozen types of IVs, a monitor for displaying X-rays and vitals, a mini fridge filled with blood and other medical supplies, and a bunch of other shit I can't name. All I need to know is that it'll work.

I just didn't expect to need it so soon.

The sliding door on the side swings open, revealing a red-faced Wren Sakovia. He wipes sweat from his brow before gesturing for Thanatos to bring Sara forward.

I raise an eyebrow at the flush across his assistant's cheeks. Do they not know how to run the AC?

While Sakovia checks Sara's vitals, his assistant notices my stare and gives it right back, giving me a once-over from head to foot. "You look good, considering."

She seems familiar.

It takes me a moment to piece together where I know her from, finally settling on a memory of her tending to my burns during my latest stint in The Box. I grunt, not really caring for her opinion. I feel fine. Achey, with some skin irritation from the net scraping against my burns and reopening a few wounds, but good overall.

This is the best I've ever felt in my life.

Considering.

When the medic—Serena, I realize, spotting the embroidered name on a duffel bag hanging over the back of the front passenger seat—sticks an IV into Sara's arm, College Girl doesn't even flinch. "I didn't numb the area," Sara mutters to herself. "What's she on? Where did you find her?"

"In the woods."

"What?" Serena's eyebrows pinch together. "What the hell was she doing in the woods?" With a shake of her head, she dismisses her own question. "Never mind. Do you know what drugs she's been given?"

"Not a clue."

Serena glares at me, like it's my fault that she's been shot up with an unidentified street drug. "Then you're dismissed." She slams the sliding door shut, leaving me staring at my reflection in the van's shiny black paint job. I don't recognize much beyond *pale, white blob*, and I'm immediately thinking of Sara again—the most recent pale, white blob that may or may not survive. Not that anyone asked for my opinion, but I have little hope that Sara will pull through. If there's one thing I'm familiar with, it's death. And this girl?

She's been marked for the grave. Once someone is marked, there's nothing mortals can do to keep them alive.

I draw in a deep breath and stare up at the clouds obscuring the half moon, painting a hazy glow in the night sky. The mountain scape lingers just below, a row of sharp teeth capped in white, glowing brighter than the clouds as the moonlight blankets the snow.

What happens next with Sara is out of our hands.

But what happens out here, in these woods, on this mountain...

With our father.

...is in our hands. I know *exactly* what I'll do when I find him. I can feel his presence in my veins, like a sickness that latches on and won't let go until you die. He hooked his claws into Sara and made her sick, too, infecting an innocent girl with his madness.

No one else has to die by his hand.

Loose gravel crunches under my boots as I turn away from the van and walk towards the woods. Thanatos calls out to me from behind, but it's easy to ignore him. All of the voices in my head—the ones ringing in my ears, the man shouting at my back, and those surfacing from the depths of my mind—blur together until all I hear is static.

There's a specific feeling that arises when I make the decision to kill someone. It's a physical sensation—a tug in the back of my skull that pulls and pulls and pulls until the space behind my eyes begins to ache, my teeth feel like they're being pushed back into my gums, and every bone in my body feels the pressure to snap. Being near Celia has lessened the tension so that I can breathe without that feeling getting in the way.

But right now, what I need most is to let that feeling in.

To let it guide me across the asphalt, beneath the

arcing branches of an unkempt forest, and into the flurries of snow turning black in the shadows.

I'm going to kill my father before he hurts anyone else.

Celia's voice suddenly cuts through the noise in my head, the image of her wide, sparkling eyes paired with the sound of her bubbling laughter as we tumble together on the trapeze net. I turn to the mountain and leave the sound of Celia's voice behind, following the general direction that Sara appeared from moments ago. I'm looking for a path that Sara might have taken down, but of course, I find none, the tracks invisible in the dark. If she descended the mountain alone, it's a miracle that she made it in one piece.

Unless she didn't travel alone.

Unless someone stripped her naked only for the final stretch.

Unless that someone is still here, lurking in the shadows, waiting for his bait to lure in a catch.

A twig snaps behind me, and I spin around to face the barrel of a sawed-off shotgun.

My blood runs cold at the wicked smile glowing in the moonlight, the man's eyes a similar shade to mine, his hair as unkempt as Emil's, his muscle mass matching Nikolai's, and his voice as deep as Thanatos's. "Let's go for a walk." His eyes flash silver in the moonlight. "*Yuri.*"

CHAPTER 23

RAGE

Sweeping Celia off of her feet is impossible with my brother in the way. "Take Ted," I tell Rebel, grinding my teeth, "and *go away.*"

He rears his head back like I've slapped him. "Why the hell would I do that?" He throws his hand out to gesture at the unconscious man lying on the ballroom floor. "I'm not dragging his ass anywhere. He fainted; he should live with the humiliation." Other guests for the gala pass us by, a few looking concerned at Ted's sorry state.

We didn't even touch him; he fainted on his own the minute we reached the bar.

"What a dumbass," Rebel continues, sighing. "Let's just leave him."

"Not on the floor." As much as I hate to admit it, Ted used to be important to Celia. We won't win any favors by treating him like garbage—even if he *is* fucking trash. I remove my jacket, drape it over the back of an armchair, and snap my fingers. "Help me lift him."

The two of us work together to set Ted on an armchair and make it look natural, like he passed out from drinking too much. I grab the first drink that passes by on a server's tray and set it down on the table beside him, the little red beach umbrella sticking out over the rim making him look even more ridiculous.

Well. Not my problem.

Rebel grabs the fruity, frozen cocktail and swallows a mouthful, then snickers as he tucks the umbrella behind Ted's ear. "Nighty-night, bitch."

We're on our way back to our table when Ruin's voice cuts back into our comms. They have a large connection radius, so we weren't worried about anyone going out-of-bounds, but somehow, Ruin has managed to test the limits of modern technology.

"Get the doctor."

I push past a meandering couple and scan the area for Ruin, not finding him, but seeing Thanatos hover at the far end of the dining platform. He's watching Celia talk with Charlotte, but he's simultaneously pulling out his cell phone to call Wren Sakovia, the doctor who agreed to work overtime to cover our asses tonight.

I have a feeling that he's looking out for Celia more than my brothers and me, but I won't complain about having another person in our corner.

"What's going on?" I take one more look around the backyard, but there aren't as many people lingering outside in the cold. Most guests are cozied up with their money and their egos indoors.

"I'll meet you at the side entrance," Thanatos tells Ruin, meeting my eyes from twenty feet away. "Rage, watch her." After one last, lingering glance at Celia, Than steps back and quickly returns indoors to meet our younger brother at the designated location.

Grabbing Rebel's forearm, I pull him forward. "C'mon. Don't let her out of your sight."

Rebel tugs his arm free. "Wasn't planning on it," he grumbles, jostling me with his elbow. "Quit pulling me around." Sighing, he rubs the side of his neck, wiping away some of the makeup covering his tattoos. It clings to his shirtsleeve, but he doesn't notice. "What do you think he's found?"

"Don't know," I answer honestly. We miss Celia's entire conversation with Charlotte, but I'm sure that sharing stories about Ted's shrimp dick wasn't very entertaining. Once we're seated at the table, Charlotte looks over her shoulder for her missing husband. "Oh, where's Ted?"

"He's sitting by the fire pit," Rebel answers, nodding toward Ted's silhouette across the lawn. "Said he wasn't hungry."

Charlotte's face pinches, and she huffs as she pushes out her seat. "I swear," she mumbles, grabbing her purse. "He takes one look at his ex and can't stand being civil." Giving us a tight-lipped smile, she excuses herself and makes a beeline for her husband.

"What did you do?" Celia hisses, jabbing my thigh with her sharp fingernail. "I didn't tell you to hurt him!"

"Relax," Rebel drawls, rolling his eyes. "He's the one doing all the damage. The bastard fainted. Can you believe it? A grown man fainting?"

I can, actually, believe it. I've seen dozens of men piss themselves—granted, they're usually tied to an interrogation chair, but still. They pass out all the time.

We can hear both Ruin and Thanatos talking in our ear, the two of them discussing exactly who it is that needs medical attention—*Sara*.

The missing college girl.

I look away from Rebel so that he doesn't give anything away. He may be flirtatious and chatty and good with people, but he does *not* lie well when he's not on the job. It's like a switch in his brain for effectiveness turns off the minute he takes a bow and walks off stage.

He needs to get better at lying, or he'll ruin every future surprise I have in store for Celia and our child.

Rebel changes the conversation, steering us away from Ted entirely. "I think one of those shows is about to start," he says, looking away from Celia to nod toward the venue. That's likely true, given how the events for the evening are scheduled to begin every hour, on the hour. "Let's go watch."

"Where did Thanatos go?" Celia asks, ignoring Rebel's suggestion completely. "He was standing right there, and then all of a sudden, he looked at me and..." Her eyebrows furrow together. "Ran off."

Thankfully, our dinner arrives, two plates of

medium-rare ribeyes paired with potatoes and broccoli and a salmon entrée completed with asparagus and rice. Rebel shoves a forkful of steaming potatoes into his mouth while I unwrap Celia's napkin and place it in her lap.

"Maybe he had to pee," Rebel muses, carving into his steak. "*Really* badly."

Celia frowns, first at Rebel, then at me. "Stop lying to me. I know that something is wrong."

"I'm not lying," Rebel replies, his ears turning pink. *Fuck me.* He will never be able to lie to Celia for as long as he lives.

She scowls at my brother before turning to face me. "My earbud isn't working. What did you do?"

Unlike Thanatos, I don't have my phone to disconnect any of our units from the system. For this part, I don't have to lie. "I didn't do anything." I hand Celia her fork. "Eat your salmon."

At least she takes a bite of her meal. "Tell me where Thanatos and Ruin are."

"They're heading back to the car," I say, trying to be honest without tipping her off.

She nibbles on a piece of asparagus. "Why?"

"Let me find out. Please eat your dinner." I unravel my own silverware and force myself to eat, hoping that she will follow suit. It's easy for Rebel; he's halfway through his plate and stealing the leftover piece of bread from Charlotte's, but my stomach clenches at the thought of Ruin finding Sara.

Where the fuck has she been hiding all this time?

Celia chews slowly, her eyes constantly roaming the lawn. I caught a flicker of movement in my peripheral as Ruin carried Sara to the side doors, but he's long gone by now, meaning that we're safe from Celia finding out that Sara is here.

If she does, there will be no stopping her from rushing to the girl's side, and acting emotionally will only make us vulnerable. We need to think clearly to process this information and decide our next steps. Let Dr. Sakovia take care of Sara; she'll be... *fine* might be a bit of a stretch, but she'll be in good hands.

I catch some of the conversation between Ruin and one of the doctors, including a brief summary of Sara's physical state and where Ruin found her... and then, silence.

Thanatos says something, but the reception crackles, making it impossible to understand. The range of our comms must be reaching its limit from one end of the venue to the other. Rebel notices, too, cutting a slice off of his steak more slowly than before as the two of us listen intently for any change.

Then, all of a sudden, Ruin starts to speak.

Our brother isn't talkative. He'd rather smoke a joint on the rooftop than engage in meaningful conversation, so his silence isn't altogether alarming. It's moments like this when he *does* speak—not to us, but to someone else —that sounds the alarm.

Something isn't right.

"You got old," he deadpans, his voice crackling in my ear. "I wish you hadn't."

What a strange thing to say.

The oddities continue as Ruin *keeps* talking, like he can't shut the fuck up. "You also gained weight. Thirty pounds. You're not balding, but you've gone gray. That limp in your right leg—is that new? No, you're overcompensating. Must be a few years old."

Our brother has never been good at conversation, but this is *bizarre.* I stand quickly and look for him, but he's not anywhere within eyesight. "Ruin," I rumble, "where are you?"

"It's cold out here," he replies, laughing. He actually *laughs.* "I left my jacket inside. You look pretty warm. You must have been out here a while."

Outside. He's outside.

Rebel joins me in looking for Ruin, except he's jogging the perimeter, scanning the lawn, then the closest side of the building. Celia taps her earpiece, then lets out a frustrated sigh. "Turn it back on!" she snaps, jumping up and latching onto my arm. "Rage!"

"I can't." I swallow my frustration. "I'm sorry."

"Sorry?" Celia stomps her foot. "Fuck your *sorry.* You're a man who gets results, so get me results. Turn it back on."

Fuck, I love this woman.

Sweeping her hair behind her ear, I gently remove her earpiece. Speaking into mine, I call for Thanatos. "Hey, turn Celia's comms back on." Acting on faith, I replace her unit with mine so that she can hear everyone's conversation, leaving me in the dark.

Her eyes widen as she listens to Ruin's awkward chatter. "Who is he talking to?"

"If I had to guess, he's talking to our dad. Or to us. Likely both."

Rebel makes a run for the trees, so I grab Celia's hand and make to follow. "Let's go." She takes her first few steps, and the click of her heels gives me pause. "Can you run in those?"

She kicks them off, daring to go barefoot. Upon seeing the skepticism on my face, she rolls her eyes and shoves past me. "C'mon! He's—he's cutting out."

They're moving further out of range.

We run across the lawn behind Rebel, my brother reaching the forest before us. He says something that I can't hear without my comms, then turns right. "He wants us to split up," Celia says from behind me. "We can go left." Just as we reach the trees, she stops and holds her hand to her ear. Her face scrunches as she listens closely. "Wait. I think I hear a car starting. They're on the road? A dirt road. It's bumpy. Ruin says that his truck is ugly." She smiles for a split second before she turns left and sprints. "The road is this way!"

I know that she's going toward the main street we took to the gala, but it's paved. If they're on a dirt road, it's not at the front of the building. It's somewhere in the back or to the side, hidden in the woods.

We have to be right next to the road. I glance up the mountain, looking for red taillights and finding none.

"He's cutting out!" Celia slows down until she comes to a stop and places both of her hands on a tree. Picking up her feet, she grimaces as she brushes them off. "They're getting too far away."

Why would my brother willingly leave with the man who's been trying to kill him for the past fifteen years? Why wouldn't he kill him as soon as he saw him?

My gaze drifts from the incline in front of me to my future wife as she runs through the underbrush, her dress snagging on fallen tree limbs, her gait slowing as she struggles to make it to the road. Following her and making faster progress than she is tugs a thread of guilt inside of my heart. She isn't built for the wilderness. A woman like Celia should be sipping on a champagne flute as fireworks light up the night sky behind her, illuminating the sparkle in her eyes.

I quickly scoop her up off the ground and cradle her in my arms. If she had been out here instead of Ruin, if our father had seen her and taken her, I would never have forgiven myself or my brothers for letting it happen. I know that Ruin would feel the same, blaming himself more than anything.

Our father has always wanted to get rid of Ruin, and Celia is collateral damage.

She closes her eyes and concentrates on what she's hearing. "Rebel is going to keep looking behind us. Thanatos is saying something about..." She pinches her bottom lip between her teeth. "Going up the mountain."

What she doesn't say is that Ruin is still talking to us, but I have no doubt that he is. We just can't hear him anymore. I take Celia's hand and give it a gentle squeeze. "He'll be okay. We'll find him."

Celia holds her breath for a long moment, then exhales heavily. "He left without saying anything. Why would he do that? Why wouldn't he fight back?" What few beads remain sewed into Celia's dress sparkle in the moonlight, a reminder of how beautiful she looked beneath the lavender spotlights an hour ago... and how my youngest brother couldn't take his eyes off of her.

In a typical scenario, Ruin would have never left with our father. He would have fought tooth and nail to kill the bastard on the spot, not caring for the damage to his own body as long as he completed the job. He would have died if it meant destroying that man.

But he would also die to keep Celia safe.

I tilt my head back and stare at the moon, the circle around it cinching tighter. A hangman's noose. An omen.

Someone is going to die tonight.

CHAPTER 24

THANATOS

WHAT MY BROTHERS don't know is that our father has nightmares. Throat-clenching, unable to breathe, night terrors. He used to wake up screaming in the middle of the afternoon, lying on a filthy mattress in broad daylight in an abandoned, run-down house in the middle of the woods.

I used to watch him suffer.

I'd get close to him while he slept, imagining all the ways he could die. Strangulation seemed too simple. Drowning was too loud. Stabbing could work, but I wanted him to bleed out for a long time, and I only had one belt that I wasn't about to sacrifice to use as a tourniquet. I thought about dousing him with gasoline and setting him on fire as a fucked-up tribute to his sins, but then his suffering would be over.

I couldn't allow my brothers' tormentor to go unpunished.

It was one thing for him to come after me. Growing

up with bruised ribs and black eyes was my induction into manhood at the ripe age of nine. But after my dad remarried and my brothers were born, our father changed. Foolishly, I thought that he might have turned a new leaf for his new favorite son Nikolai and his perfect wife who provided him with such a gifted heir. Even after Emil was born, our father attended t-ball games, barbecued on the back porch on the weekends, and kept his shady business deals under wraps so that my step-mother could answer honestly when the police came knocking with questions.

But once my youngest brother Yuri was born, everything changed. I'm not sure what tipped our father over the edge—the way his mother would sing Russian lullabies to stop him from crying, or how he lost his job at the meat-packing plant when they shut down an entire factory, or the phone call from one of the bratva's *vors* at the time, saying that he needed to pick up slack in our part of town and start contributing to the Baranova's legacy.

I don't think he ever anticipated becoming a made man. The previous *pakhan* Tolkotsky was known for his obsession with bloodlines, and ours was so watered down that our father never got the call to officially join the bratva's ranks. It wasn't until a skirmish at the city's borders took out a few dozen men that Tolkotsky started recruiting from the dredges of Russian society—even going so far as to induct orphans from the *Harlin Heights Home for Children.*

Sometimes, I think that Ezra and Andrei were lucky

not to know their parents. At least when they look in the mirror, they won't have to see every fatal flaw their parents passed down staring back at them.

As I watched my father's body seize up in blind terror on that dirty mattress over and over again, I wondered if I would end up like him. Choking on my own spit, unable to break out of whatever nightmare I'd created.

I have no doubt that he smells my step-mother's charred flesh in his dreams.

He fucking deserves that memory. The rest of us have to live with the remains of our unhappy childhood and subsequent descent into aggression as an outlet. I took to brawling in the streets when I was a teenager. That's how I met Ezra, the two of us climbing the bratva ranks in record time. It's why I wasn't there when our house burned down; I was beating the shit out of some lowlife who hadn't paid his protection fees.

Like my brothers, I'm good at violence.

But that doesn't mean that I enjoy it.

My father's pain, on the other hand, is the one crucial exception. A year or two ago, he finally noticed that I was following him and tried to flee, so I shot him in the leg and fractured his femur. As he crawled to a hospital and later claimed a local Catholic Church as sanctuary, I waited for him to run again.

I waited so long that I got careless, letting him slip back into the city like a rat returning to its hole.

It's my fault that he noticed my brothers' dedicated attention to Celia, because I'm the one that failed to kill him before he could come crawling back. When I first returned to the city, I thought that I could rejoin the bratva and reunite with my brothers so that we could kill our dad together. In a sense, I wasn't wrong —but I wasn't entirely right, either. All three of them were distracted by the pretty girl with tears in her eyes and a fire in her heart. Inevitably, we would kill our dad —but what was the rush when he wasn't doing us any harm?

It was stupid to underestimate him, and now, we're paying the price. We've *been* paying for weeks, between all the dead girls and the threats on our family, until now— this very moment when our youngest brother slips from our grasp, right beneath our noses.

Was I not calculated enough?

Fast enough?

Did I let Ruin walk away from me too quickly, or was I too focused on getting the girl to safety to realize what my brother was planning?

Have I been too blinded by beauty to recognize its cost, or did I think that, no matter the sacrifice, it would be worth a taste of her lips?

I clench my fists as I watch an old, beat-up, red pickup truck tumble down a dirt road that spirals up the mountainside, one of the truck's taillights flickering as the bulb threatens to blow. Ruin is in that truck—but so is our father.

The bastard *has* to die tonight.

I slide into the driver's seat of Rage's SUV and turn the key, revving the engine and hitting the gas to follow the truck. It turns on another dirt road, this one cutting a straight path across the mountain. We aren't going to the snow-capped ski cliffs like most people do.

We're heading for the half dozen natural springs dotting the hills, each one hosting a simple log cabin built decades ago to increase tourism to the area. Local college kids rent them out for orgies and hazings, but otherwise, they're in decline, the beach scene in the summer and the ski lodge in the winter stealing nearly all of Harlin Heights' tourism.

Our father must have known that the cabins lay empty most of the year. He also must have known that dropping bodies in back alleys and behind sand dunes on the beach would keep our attention inside city limits, rather than have us explore the outskirts in search of him.

For a man who pisses alcohol and wets the bed, he's been strategic ever since he returned to the city.

Which means that in order to beat him, we have to be twice as smart.

I keep my headlights off as their vehicle pulls up to one of the cabins, the police tape blocking the driveway having been broken long before our arrival. Somehow, it both drags in the mud and flaps in the icy breeze, a testament to how little the city's police force cares about its citizens' safety. I doubt they properly cleared the scene if my father has been holing up here for weeks.

My father drives right past the broken caution tape, clearly not intimidated in the slightest by the police's potential presence in the area, and parks around back, out of sight.

Pulling my phone from my pocket, I pin my location

for my brothers to find, turn off the SUV, and step into the cold night air. Snow gently falls overhead, dusting the trees in white powder. It melts as it hits the ground, but it hovers over the spring's glassy surface, tricking the naked eye into thinking that it's solid.

I move on, not caring for the cold or the snow, determined to meet my father where he stands. I could pull out my gun and shoot him in the head, but we all agreed that Ruin would claim the kill.

If Ruin *wanted* to kill him, however, he would have already done so. What is he waiting for? An invitation?

The front door of the cabin is unlocked when I turn the handle, and I let myself inside. It's dark, the living room eerily quiet. I pull my handgun from my waistband and carefully clear the room, moving methodically through the space in search of my father or brother. When I reach the back of the house, I realize that they aren't inside—they're in the underground basement, the outdoor hatch left wide open so that dull, orange light beams into the night sky.

It's clearly a trap, but what choice do I have?

My brother is only in danger because of my failures. I can't hesitate any longer. Playing judge *and* executioner hasn't yielded any tangible results. It's time to end this for good.

Slowly, I drop down into the musty, damp pit, the wooden steps creaking as I descend. A pungent, rotten stench fills my nose the deeper I go, and I hold my breath as I reach the landing.

My brother is sitting in a metal folding chair in the

middle of the room, unbound and unarmed, his favorite hunting knife missing from his hip. He stares unflinchingly ahead as our father flicks a Zippo lighter behind Ruin's back, the flame snapping on and off with each jerk of his wrist.

"Thanatos," my father greets, a sinister smile curving across his lips. "Here to say goodbye to your brother?"

I was expecting to find the same man I've been watching deteriorate for the past few years, but my father looks *good*—healthy, even. His hair isn't greasy or unkempt; he's styled it and combed it away from his face. Clean-shaven and wearing a crisp white t-shirt and faded blue jeans that make him look ten years younger. He fiddles with a poker chip in his left hand, the only nervous tic I can find. A hunting jacket lay discarded on the back of a second folding chair, with a double-barrel shotgun resting on the table in front of it. Along the side wall, a cork board covered in dirty instruments catches my eye, each of the tools rusted over.

A whiff of copper fills my nose as I mistakenly take a breath, and only then do I notice the reddish stains coating the board, the rust having long since dried into a fine powder. Except, some of the stains are fresh, having dripped onto the worn workbench sitting below...

I clench my jaw and steady the unease churning in my gut, because that's not *rust*.

My father's gaze snaps to mine, the man unflinchingly confident as he takes in my appearance. "You didn't happen to bring a pretty brunette with you? No?" He clicks his tongue against his teeth. "I was telling Yuri how much I wanted to see her again. She's quite a beauty, isn't she? Your girl." The last bit he says to Ruin, but my brother doesn't respond.

It's like he's gone mute after talking nonstop on the drive over, his social battery run dry.

"You know," our father continues, placing his hands on Ruin's shoulders, "I really am disappointed in you boys. All that fucking, and you still couldn't knock her up." His smile glints in the orange light. "I bet I could get her pregnant. My swimmers are *strong*. I have four sons as proof of that." He pulls something out from behind his back, and the flash of silver makes my stomach drop.

Ruin's hunting knife isn't missing—it's stolen.

Holding the knife to Ruin's throat, my father's face twitches into the one I recognize—the unhinged maniac finally coming out to play. He cracks his neck with a quick jerk of his head, then exhales. "Well, I have three sons and one *mistake*." A tiny line of red appears on Ruin's skin, the knife having made a new incision on top of the one that Celia left earlier this evening. He bends to whisper into Ruin's ear. "But all mistakes can be corrected."

Ruin finally looks up at me, and I can see the decision in their depths. He's going to kill our father... but he's waiting for something first.

We don't have time to wait.

"Hold on," I call out, keeping my gun trained ahead. "Just hold on. Let's talk."

Maybe I can stall for time—

The knife digs deeper, making Ruin wince.

Fuck.

"What if we trade?" My heart hammers inside my chest as adrenaline kicks through my system. I swallow, knowing that what I'm about to propose will piss my brothers off...and undoubtedly sign my own death warrant.

But I'll do anything to save my brothers from this bastard.

Even break their hearts.

"Give me Yuri," I say slowly, lowering my gun, "and I'll get you what you really want. *Who* you really want." Searing pain wracks my nervous system as my heart and my head war with each other. Even Ruin, motionless until now, glares at me.

If I go through with this, I'm moving to the top of Ruin's hit list. Quite frankly, I'll deserve it and every second of Hell that awaits me.

The truth is, we've all wanted the same thing from the start: Celia Monrovia, the prettiest girl in the bratva. Our father is no exception, although he doesn't want to keep her for himself...

He wants to torture and kill her.

A life for a life—our mother's for Celia's. A fair trade, in our father's eyes.

I can't force air into my lungs as guilt swallows me whole. Somehow, I manage to say the words that will bring not only my downfall, but my entire family's ruin.

"I'll give you Celia if you give me Yuri. *Alive.*"

My father's wickedness spreads like a wildfire, consuming every flicker of humanity dwelling within him until there's nothing left but a devil grinning at his prey.

"You have yourself a deal."

Claim your revenge in book four, Born to Riot.

Thank you so much for reading *Bound by Ruin!* Please leave a rating or review if you enjoyed spending time with these trauma boys. 🖤

Want to learn more about the Baranova Bratva and where Riot gets his name? Dive into *Rule of Three* in ebook, paperback, or Kindle Unlimited. Amazon US

About the Author

Just a smut-lover listening to angsty love songs on repeat.

Misti Wilds loves watching characters pine after one another from afar--until a tall, dark, brooding alpha male says *fuck this* and claims his woman. But one man isn't enough these days--Misti's got her hands full when it comes to writing multiple dark and delicious men with violence in their hearts and a declaration of love etched on the barrel of their guns.

Why choose one when you can have them all?

Also by Misti Wilds

Baranova Bratva:

Rule of Three

Reign of Four

Brutal Beauty:

Brutal Beauty (prequel)

Claimed by Rage

Tempted to Rebel

Bound by Ruin

Born to Riot

Serial Killer Romance:

Begging for Mercy